C'Yani & Meek

A Dangerous Hood Love

Tina J

Copyright 2020

More Books by Tina J

A Thin Line Between Me & My Thug 1-2
I Got Luv for My Shawty 1-2
Kharis and Caleb: A Different kind of Love 1-2
Loving You is a Battle 1-3
Violet and the Connect 1-3
You Complete Me
Love Will Lead You Back
This Thing Called Love
Are We in This Together 1-3
Shawty Down to Ride For a Boss 1-3
When a Boss Falls in Love 1-3
Let Me Be The One 1-2
We Got That Forever Love
Ain't No Savage Like The One I got 1-2
A Queen & Hustla 1-3 (collab)
Thirsty for a Bad Boy 1-2
Hasaan and Serena: An Unforgettable Love 1-2
We Both End Up With Scars
Caught up Luvin a beast 1-3
A Street King & his Shawty 1-2
I Fell for the Wrong Bad Boy 1-2 (collab)
Addicted to Loving a Boss 1-3
All Eyes on the Crown 1-3
I Need that Gangsta Love 1-2 (collab)
Still Luvin' a Beast 1-2
Creepin' With The Plug 1-2
I Wanna Love You 1-2
Her Man, His Savage 1-2
When She's Bad, I'm Badder 1-3
Marco & Rakia 1-3
Feenin' for a Real One 1-3
A Kingpin's Dynasty 1-3
What Kind Of Love Is This?
Frankie & Lexi 1-3
A Dope Boy's Seduction 1-3
My Brother's Keeper 1-3
C'Yani & Meek 1-3

Warning:

This book is strictly Urban Fiction and the story is **NOT**

REAL!

Characters will not behave the way you want them to; nor will

they react to situations the way you think they should. Some of

them may be drug addicts, kingpins, savages, thugs, rich, poor,

ho's, sluts, haters, bitter ex-girlfriends or boyfriends, people

from the past and the list can go on and on. That is what Urban

Fiction mostly consists of. If this isn't anything you foresee

yourself interested in, then do yourself a favor and don't read it

because it's only going to piss you off. ☺☺

Also, the book will not end the way you want so please be

advised that the outcome will be based solely on my own

thoughts and ideas Thanks so much to my readers, supporters,

publisher and fellow authors and authoress for the support.

Author Tina J

Prologue 2016…

Meek

I walked in my house and glanced at the photos with me and my ex Kim. This is the woman I planned on marrying and having babies with. Unfortunately, after two years of what I thought would end up perfect, ended up the exact opposite.

In the beginning, her confidence was at an all-time high. There wasn't any woman out here who could hold a torch to her. She held it down in all ways possible and it was no need for me to stray. Not that I would because my mother taught me better than that. Plus, I didn't want karma to hit me back worse.

During the last six months of our relationship, she became more territorial and the accusations were outta this world. For instance, I could be downstairs sleep and my dick could've been semi hard from having to use the bathroom. This chick would say I dreamt about another woman and fucked her in my dream.

Another time, I was showering at her house and she came home with her sister. I exit the bathroom in just a towel and she accused me of wishing her sister was the one in the room. I can't even tell you how many made up stories she came up with in her head. I should've known then she was looney but I gave her the benefit of the doubt of being overprotective.

The reason I broke up with her is because of that and she was being too clingy. I couldn't go anywhere without checking in. I felt like she portrayed my mother and I was her kid more than anything.

Don't get me wrong; sexually she's perfect and we had our good times. But the longer you're with someone, the more you'll start to see their true colors. Everything she kept hidden began to surface and a nigga was fed up.

"Ahhhhh." I heard and ran up the steps only to find the same woman I left a few months ago, on the bedroom floor bleeding. The windows were broken and glass was everywhere. My first instinct was to ask questions but with the amount of blood she had pouring out, I ran to grab a towel.

"What happened?" I'm confused as fuck on why she's here because I took my key back and we hadn't spoken. It didn't dawn on me that she most likely made a copy but she had to in order to get inside.

"Meek, I waited for you. Where have you been?" I wrapped her arm up and noticed the bruises on her face and the crooked nose.

"Did someone break in here? Why are my windows broke?" She didn't say a word and ran her good hand down the side of my face.

"POLICE FREEZE!" I turned around and about ten cops busted in the room. I kid you not.

"Freeze my ass. She needs help and why the fuck are you barging in my house? Who called you?"

"Sir, we need you to stand up and put your hands behind your back."

"What the fuck for? This my shit."

"Sir, I'm not going to ask again." I looked and each cop had a gun pointed at me. I did like he asked and stared at Kim who was being treated by an EMT that walked in. A woman cop sat next to her and began rubbing her shoulders.

"Kim what's going on?"

"You have the right to remain silent." I listened to the cop read me my rights and continued staring at my ex.

"I told him we couldn't be together because of his hand problem." The female cop glanced up at me and rolled her eyes.

"HOLD THE FUCK UP! BITCH WHAT DID YOU TELL THEM?" The cop started pushing me out the door.

"Meek, I'm sorry but I couldn't take another beating."

"Tha fuck you just say?" I was confused as hell. I've never in my life put my hands on a woman but she had me ready to kill her. I tried to break free and they wrestled me to the ground.

"Meek, don't fight them."

"YOU TOLD THEM I DID THIS?" I shouted again. By now, I'm fuming and nothing could calm me down.

"It's ok baby. You're gonna get the help you need." She let tears fall down her face and rested her head on the officer's arm. She was milking the shit outta them.

"If you continue to fight, we'll have to tase you." I tried to relax but it was hard hearing her accuse me of abusing her.

8

"Fuck this. That bitch lying." The cop walked me down the steps and pushed my head down to get in the backseat of his car.

The door opened on the opposite side and my boy Cliff, who I did business with sat next to me. He had one leg hanging out and I was shocked to see the cops allowing him to talk but then again, he is the mayor.

When I first came to town, I already had my license to start a construction company but it was in California. My grandfather, who is the reverend everyone loved, set up a meeting with him to expedite the process. I thought he'd be a tight ass because of his color and actually he was more down to earth than I thought.

We hit it off right away and ended up having a four-hour meeting discussing the future possibilities. Ever since then, he's sent business my way and I had money to blow. I'm very appreciative of him but he also knows I won't kiss his ass or no one else's. He may have sent people my way, but I'm still the one who landed the deals.

"What happened?" I stared at my house and shook my head.

"Man, I come home from work and hear Kim upstairs yelling."

"Kim? I thought you broke up with her." He gave me a crazy look because he knew like everyone else, I broke up with her.

"I did. I took my key, changed my phone number and everything."

"How did she get in?"

"She must've made a copy. FUCK! I should've been on top of that." I rested my head on the seat.

"Anyway, I go upstairs and not only is she bleeding and her face fucked up but the windows are broke in my house." I shook my head in disgust.

"You sure, you didn't do it."

"If I did, she wouldn't have been able to contact the cops." I gave him a look and he nodded.

"You have blood all over your clothes, that's why I asked."

"Cliff, I was with her for two years. I come in to find her bleeding, of course I'm gonna run to her. It didn't even dawn on me to be careful. All the blood made me think she was dying and I don't want that. Well I didn't. Now she can burn in hell for all I care."

"Don't you have cameras?"

"Yea. I'm gonna have my lawyer come get me and give him the video."

"Good. You're a good guy and I don't want you losing all you worked for over some bullshit." That's why I liked Cliff. He was an older white man who didn't give a fuck about what no one said. If he rocked with you, he'd have your back no matter what. However; I understood his position and respected his hustle, the same as he did mine.

"How did you know what happened?" I asked as he stepped out.

"I was up late working and heard your address over the scanner. When they said domestic violence is the reason, I knew something wasn't right." I didn't say anything.

"Let him make as many phone calls as he needs." The cop nodded.

"If he has one scratch or bruise on him, you'll be hearing from me." He shouted to each cop.

"Call me tomorrow so we can discuss some new prospects."

"A'ight." He patted the top of the police car and walked off. As the car pulled off I saw them bringing Kim out in a stretcher. This bitch is crazier than I thought.

****

"This is a temporary restraining order against her. Here is the court date to file a permanent one." The woman at the front desk of the courthouse said. My lawyer requested me to get it because he claims if Kim did something this crazy, it's no telling what else she'll do.

"Thank you." I took the paper out her hand and looked at my lawyer.

"I feel like a bitch doing this."

"Look at it this way." He glanced around to see if anyone was paying attention.

12

"This is protecting you in case other things need to happen." We both knew what he spoke of.

"Excuse me." A chick said and stepped on the elevator. Shorty was bad and I caught myself staring. The elevator bell rung for us to step off and the woman grabbed my hand.

"I saw you in the mirror staring." She pointed to the one above us.

"Call me." She pulled a card out her purse and handed it to me.

"We'll see." I stepped off and noticed the card had her cell and house number on it. What stood out the most is her name. It read Theresa AKA Tasty. I bet she's a stripper. Not that I mind because I'm not looking for a woman after this shit.

I put the number in my phone and made plans to hit her up. I'm damn sure gonna need to fuck and I hope she ain't on no dumb shit because I'll keep it moving. From here on out I just want a bitch to suck and fuck me. If I meet a woman in the process she's gonna have to do a lot to prove she ain't as crazy as Kim.

"What the fuck?" My lawyer parked in my driveway. We got out and all four of my tires were flat, the windows were broken, spray painted words was on one side and all my downstairs windows were gone. I shook my head and my lawyer did the same.

"Let's get the tape." We went inside and besides the windows being broke everything else is still in place.

I went in my office and didn't have to say a word. The entire place was fucked up. The computer was missing and so was my laptop. I'm glad nothing important is on it. However; the video is so I know Kim is responsible. I'm glad she's out my life and if I ever see her again she better hope I don't kill her. *Stupid bitch.*

Present Day…

C'Yani "Cee" Bailey

"He's not answering C'Yani. We can't wait." My mom said and helped me to the car. Here I am nine months pregnant and my boyfriend, or should I say fiancé is nowhere to be found as usual.

"How long are you gonna stick around knowing what he's doing?" I laid my head on the headrest and closed my eyes. The contractions were kicking my ass and she's discussing me leaving Tyrone.

The guy she's speaking of has been my man for the last five years. We were happy or so I thought. We both had money, great positions at our job, took vacations together and so forth. In my eyes, if you spoke of the perfect couple you had to be talking about us. He could do no wrong and I hated to believe he was but the evidence stared me in the face everyday.

He's been MIA a lot lately and as bad as I may not want to admit it, he's cheating. The woman calls all hours of the night, sends text messages and he's even gone away for weeks at a time with this person. I know it's what I get for staying but when you've become comfortable with a man, you tend to think he'll eventually stop messing around and come home but not Ty. He does whatever he wants and I don't say a word but if he misses my son's birth, we are officially over. Some things I can ignore, however; this moment only happens once.

"I know where he is and if she's more important that our child then it's his fault he'll miss the birth." I clutched the door handle and middle console as the pain ripped through me again.

"Sweetie, I don't want to be a bother but what you're allowing him to do isn't acceptable. You're a gorgeous woman and any man would be happy to have you on his arm."

"Just not him, right?" I snapped. I wasn't mad at her but she didn't know when to stop. Moms always wanna make you feel better but she made me feel worse. Ty ain't shit but he's my man and I'm the only one who should have an issue with the things he's doing.

"C'Yani, I know you get upset when I mention it but you are my daughter and I hate seeing you hurt." She glanced over and noticed my face.

"Breathe honey. Breathe." The tears were running down my face as she finally pulled up to the hospital.

"Let me get a nurse." She parked and ran in. A nurse returned with a wheelchair, opened the door and helped me get in.

"I'll be right up C'Yani. Let me park." I nodded and gripped the sides of the chair.

The nurse pressed the elevator and kept saying it would be fine. How did she know? Was she inside my belly feeling the pain? Again, I wasn't mad at her but she too felt my wrath. Each second passing and my fiancé wasn't here only infuriated me more and sad to say, I was taking it out on everyone.

When the elevator opened, she pushed me to the desk and asked them what room to put me in. Another nurse came and took me down the hall. As I stood, something trickled down my leg. Both of us looked and the amount of blood told me there's a problem. She pressed the button and had me hurry to the bed.

"GET A DOCTOR IN HERE NOW!" She shouted when someone asked what she needed on the intercom. Twenty seconds later a doctor and more nurses rushed in and they too had a somber look. But why? Is it more blood then what I previously saw?

"Is my baby ok?" A woman pushed the ultra sound machine in and the doctor rushed to look. He finished, put gloves on and had everyone prepare for my delivery. I didn't even know my body dilated. My mother came running in and grabbed my hand.

"Daddy's on his way." I nodded and began pushing like the doctor told me.

"I see the head. Keep pushing." After twenty minutes of doing so, I felt much better down below.

"Why isn't my baby crying?" I stared at the doctor and nurses. He placed my child in the crib and a nurse rushed out. Instead of answering me, he told me I had to be stitched up due to a tear.

"Where's my baby?" I asked and he continued ignoring me.

"WHERE THE HECK IS MY CHILD?" I shouted and told him I was getting up if he didn't speak. A minute later, a woman dressed up in a two-piece suit stepped in, nodded and after stitching me up, he left out.

"How are you Ms. Bailey?" She stood at the foot of my bed.

"Don't patronize me. Where's my baby?" I wasn't stupid. If they rushed my child out obviously something is wrong.

"I'm sorry Ms. Bailey but your child didn't make it." My eyes grew wide.

"Excuse me."

"When you delivered, your son was stillborn."

"No. No. No. I went to the doctors last week and he was fine." I was shaking my head in disbelief and felt my mother squeezing my hand.

"Ms. Bailey, these things happen and even though your appointment was good, the baby could've passed away

19

afterwards. Did you feel him kick at all in the last few days?"
My mom looked at me.

"Well no. I don't know. I wasn't paying attention. I've been so stressed and preparing myself for his arrival, it slipped my mind." My mom put her head down.

"It could've happened at any time Ms. Bailey."

"No. I had contractions and the doctor checked me before I delivered. He didn't say anything was wrong. You're lying. Where's my child?"

"Your father is with him right now."

"How is my father with him?"

"He was standing outside the door as you delivered."

"I told you he was coming honey. He probably didn't want to see you in pain. You know how he is." My mom said and I still sat there in disbelief hearing my son didn't make it.

"As far as the doctor goes, they don't inform the mom anymore until it's over because they refuse to push out a stillborn child. In doing that, it makes things harder."

"What?"

"The doctor stated when you arrived, you lost a tremendous amount of blood..." I cut her off.

"Please don't tell me I lost my child." Tears welled in my eyes as I begged her in so many words to say its not true.

"I'm sorry Ms. Bailey. When you're ready the nurse will take you to see him and say your goodbyes."

"Ma please tell me it's not true." When my father stepped in wiping his eyes, I knew then the unthinkable happened. He ran to my side and held me tight.

None of us spoke for a half hour until my sister walked in. My father told her what happened and it was like a crying fest in here.

"Get yourself together C'Yani so we can go see him." My mom spoke in a firm tone. She wasn't angry but I had to see him now, so the staff could take the necessary steps to do whatever's next.

"Daddy are you sure it's my son?" I questioned because people were stealing babies and some would say they passed and it's not true. I prayed he told me it wasn't.

"Girl please. He'd probably do me just as bad, if not worse." She stopped and stared at me.

"Sis don't let the streets fool you. There are some good, hood niggas out there looking for corny women like you."

"To run all over me." She lifted my face.

"Not to run over you but for you to make them better. Believe it or not, men aren't looking for the ratchet, hood rats anymore. They want a good woman who will match their fly, have intelligent conversation and have something going for themselves. Corny or not sis, you are all those things and a man will be happy to have you by his side."

"But sex."

"Girl that's another story. You have to deal with that when it happens." The two of us busted out laughing. It's obvious I'm not a virgin but I don't know what it's like to have that explosive sex women speak of and hopefully a man will show me one day because Ty sure didn't.

"Shit, I swear you can suck some dick." I pulled

Jasmine up and tongued her down. She got me hard again and

bent down with her legs spread apart.

"Fuck me Ty." She looked back with her index finger

in her mouth. I pushed my way in her tight pussy and stopped.

I noticed my phone going off and glanced to see it was C'Yani.

I thought about answering it because she's pregnant but her

due date isn't for another two weeks so I'm good.

"Must be your bitch." Jasmine snapped.

"What I tell you about that?" I pulled out and rammed

myself harder inside.

It's no secret she's my side chick and can't stand my

fiancé. I can't tell you how many times I had to stop her from

going to my house, calling her or even exposing who she is.

The shit pissed me off more than once and I told her if she

threatened to do it again, we're over.

C'Yani knows I'm not faithful and has tried to leave me

various times, however; I'm one of those stingy men who

wanted my cake and eat it too. Therefore; I wasn't giving her up. I mean why should I? She's beautiful, has a great job, money out the ass and will cater to my every need.

C'Yani is gorgeous standing at five foot five with hips and ass to die for. Her light brown eyes always did something to me and it's one of the reasons I fell for her. The way she looked at me made my heart skip a beat. I don't know if it's because I know how much she loves me or what.

Her appearance is always on point and she never came outta character unless necessary. I guess her bougie ass parents raised her that way. They should've told her to look in the mirror because regardless of them being white; she's black.

I'm not saying she had to be ghetto but she hangs around no black women, doesn't associate herself with going to clubs or any other place with black people or anything. I ain't never seen nothing like it. Matter of fact, I don't recall her even dining out in a place like Red Lobster, Chili's or places like that. I'm all for living good but she is on a different level.

If you're wondering why I dip out, that's easy. She's boring in the bedroom. We can only do it missionary style, she doesn't suck dick and barely lets me go down on her. I have no idea why she doesn't explore other options and after years of the same thing, I started seeking better sex elsewhere.

And yes, I have spoken with her about doing other things in the bedroom and she shuts me down every time. I didn't really dwell on it much but I got tired of hearing myself talk and left it alone. I would've never stepped out had she been willing to try new things and I can't go back now.

"I'm sorry daddy." I smacked her ass and watched it jiggle.

"You better be." I grabbed her ass cheeks and dug deeper. Now Jasmine is Spanish and just as pretty. She reminded me of a younger version of J-Lo.

I met her at one of the clubs. She was a stripper and bottle girl. I say was because she no longer works there. Side chick or not, I'm not about to have her allowing men to touch her and see what's mine. Both of us are STD free and I'm gonna keep it that way, especially; when I have a woman. I can't be bringing her home anything.

went on vacations. I'm sure she's bothered to hear another woman around me.

"You're still on the phone. Ty, this is our vacation." She whined and my mother was pissed, cursed me out an hung up.

"Let's go in here." She led me in some female lingerie store. I told her to give me a minute, stepped back outside and called C'Yani.

"The number you dialed is no longer in service." I glanced at my phone to make sure I dialed the correct number. I hit it again and the operator repeated the same. I pressed the button to call the house and it was the same thing. I ran in the store and snatched Jasmine up.

"We gotta go."

"Why?" She looked confused.

"Something happened to C'Yani. I have to make sure she's alright." She sucked her teeth and started talking shit. I pushed her against the wall outside and spoke firmly in her ear.

"You agreed to be my side chick, and with that you have a position to play." She rolled her eyes. I grabbed her chin and forced her to look at me.

"You get just about the same privileges she gets in being with me so cut the bullshit."

"But we have two more days to be here."

"Ok and if I tell you my girl may be hurt then you shut the fuck up and do what I say."

"Tyrone."

"Nah fuck that. Your ass about to be on knock off if you keep doing the shit." I walked away with her following.

I loved Jasmine but these childish ways of hers got on my nerves. If it were C'Yani, I wouldn't care because she's my girl but Jasmine gotta chill.

I didn't say two words to her on the way back to the hotel. We got in the room and started packing.

"I'm sorry. I just want you to myself when we're away. But every time she finds a way to distract you."

"You have me all to yourself Jasmine but whether you like it or not, she will always be first." She stopped and looked at me.

"Well I guess both of our kids will be before either of us." I froze.

"Yea I'm pregnant. Three months to be exact and there's no time to terminate it so don't ask." I fell against the wall. I had no one to blame but myself.

"You should've told me sooner."

"Why so you could make me get rid of it?"

"Maybe. You know what? I can't do this no more." I grabbed my bag and headed for the door.

"Wait! I'm not pregnant. I was just saying it to keep you." I snapped my neck to look at her.

"I have the thing in my arm." She showed me her arm and it was something in it. I can't tell you if it's the truth but I was able to breathe again. I don't know how I would've explained another child to my girl.

"Jasmine we should take a break. I can't keep.-"

"Nope. You're stuck with me baby." She never gave me a chance to respond as her mouth wrapped around my dick. Here we are supposed to be leaving and about to get it popping. Oh well. I'll see my girl in two days.

I sat at my desk thinking about my piece of shit fiancé and broke down crying. I know he went away for business and pleasure I'm sure, but to know he couldn't answer the phone for me only proves we don't belong together. Granted, I don't usually call when he's away, and because I did it should've been a dead giveaway something wasn't right. Yet; here it is three days later and not one peep from him. I did change my phone numbers but the one at my job is the same.

The day I left the hospital without my child, I was devastated. My mom caught me just in time from taking pills. In my eyes, there wasn't anything to live for. Later on that day, Teri came over and helped me move out because the thought of living there with no child was too heartbreaking. All of the things in my sons' room were a constant reminder of his loss and I couldn't take it.

I was so in love with my child and couldn't wait to deliver, only to be hit with losing him. I wanted to die just to take care of him in heaven. I guess God had other plans but why? Did he leave me here to suffer? How does a woman go

34

on after losing a child? No matter what the situation or age, it's a loss a mother shouldn't go through.

The social service woman asked if I wanted to bury him. I told her no and let my parents do it. They dressed him in one of the outfits I had for him to go home in and took pictures. There was no service and I refused to let them burn his tiny body. At least, I would be able to visit him at the cemetery.

The doctor told me not to return to work for at least three weeks. But again, why would I stay home when there's no child? I'm experiencing pain, however; I can't stay in the house.

"Are you ok?" Teri asked and walked in my office. I gave her a half a smile but she knew it was fake. She sat down in front of me and I stared at how pretty she was. We resembled each other a little and if you didn't know our background, you'd think we had the same parents but nope. See, both of us were adopted by the Baileys and blood couldn't make us more related.

We did everything together and even though she's ten times more hood and ghetto than me, I love her just the same.

35

She's carefree and doesn't care about anyone talking about her, where I've been struggling to keep this uppity image. It's not like anyone's forcing me but the business I'm in, makes me look the other way a lot and it's made me immune to my actions.

What I mean is, I'm the only black woman in a high position of this Advertising firm. I've dealt with racism, sexism and any other *ism* you can think of. It's crazy because I'm nothing like people assume.

Do I like nice things? Absolutely! The Baileys raised us expecting nothing but the best, which is why we each have an extensive bank account and went to Ivy League schools.

My mom inherited millions from her grandparents when she was young and opened a few businesses. Over time they grew, she met my father and they invested more; becoming richer. Unfortunately, they couldn't have kids which is where we came in.

I was adopted first and six months later Teri came. We have a little brother they adopted at birth, who is four now and he is the love of my life too. He is always with me and Teri and if not, he's begging to come be with us. Our parents are only in their late 40's but you'd never know looking at them.

Anyway, I moved in with my sister, changed all my numbers and wrote Ty off. It's in my best interest anyway. I knew he was cheating but I thought he'd get over it and realize no woman is like me but nope. He's not gonna change and if I continue to take him back, it's going to keep happening.

"I'm fine. Thinking about him that's all." I turned the 8 by 10 frame on my desk around with the ultrasound and burial photo in it.

"C, you shouldn't even be here but since you are, first things first." She took the picture off my desk.

"What are you doing?" I stood and went to get it.

"I'm only putting it over here relax." She put her arm out to keep me away and placed the frame on the book case.

"It's not to make you forget but if he's always in your face, more breakdowns are guaranteed to come. Next." She moved me to my seat.

"Sis, I'm going to take you out. Jasmine and I are going to this new club..." Soon as she mentioned her friend my face changed.

That woman couldn't stand me for some reason and I had no clue as to why. Her and my sister were friends from college. We used to be cool but over the last year, she gave me her ass to kiss or should I say tried because I didn't care if she spoke.

I'll never understand why a woman with a degree in sociology turned to stripping. The money is good from what I hear but who wants men feeling all over and disrespecting them?

"Jasmine's cool sis. I don't know why she changed up on you but fuck her. It's about you moving on without Ty." I felt tears welling in my eyes when she mentioned him.

"Why didn't he answer the phone Teri? Our baby died and he was with that woman. Did he hate me that much?" Whoever the chick is he cheated with, had him doing more disappearing acts than usual.

"Fuck him C. You deserve so much better." I nodded my head yes.

"Ms. Bailey, your appointment is here." My secretary Jenny chimed in on the intercom. She's probably the only person around I'd consider my friend besides my sister. She's down to earth, funny and doesn't go out either because she has a kid. I don't tell her all my business but she knows a little. Teri rose out of the chair and gave me a hug.

"Eat the food I brought and I'll see you later." She pointed to the tray on my desk.

I didn't even pay it no mind when she came. She walked out and I told my secretary to give me five minutes to scarf down this food. I hadn't eaten in days but Teri knew bringing me soul food would definitely make me. I opened the tray and saw cornbread, greens, baked Mac and cheese and fried chicken. *She's the best.* I tore the food up and called my client in. Mr. Gibson stepped in and we got straight to work.

****

"C'Yani." I heard his voice and continued walking up to my sister's house, well mine too now.

39

"Oh, you not speaking to me?" I stopped and turned. Did he really have the audacity to ask me that?

"Ugh, why is your stomach smaller than when I left a week ago?" His mother must not have mentioned it. I stormed in his direction and pushed him in the chest. I'm not violent, don't know how to fight and barely curse so what I wanted to do, I couldn't.

"Why didn't you answer the phone Ty? Was she that important? Why didn't you just answer?" I pounded on his chest over and over until he took both wrist in his hands.

"I'm sorry baby." I snatched away.

"Sorry huh?" He looked at my belly. It's still a little pouch there but not as big as when my child was in there.

"Did you have my son?" I dropped to the ground and began to cry hysterically. The mention of him had me doing that a lot.

"C'Yani talk to me." It took me a few minutes to get together.

I looked at him and all I wanted was for him to be in love with me, the way I was in love with him but his eyes told

40

a different story. One that says he no longer feels the same. I stood and went to the door, unlocked it and turned to him.

"While you were laid up sleeping with your side chick and doing God knows what, our child was dying in my stomach."

"WHAT?" He came closer.

"I called a hundred times and you didn't answer. I needed you Ty and once again you left me to fend for myself."

"Where's my son C'Yani?"

"In the cemetery."

"The cemetery?" He questioned like he didn't believe me. Why would I lie about something like that?

"I laid in the hospital bed and pushed out a dead baby. A baby whose father was so engrossed in another woman he couldn't even see him come out or better yet, get buried. I hate you Ty and I'll never forgive you." I slammed the door in his face and dropped again. He banged on the door for a good five minutes begging me to open it but I couldn't. There's no comforting me anymore. When I needed him he wasn't there.

I balled up in a fetal position and cried for my child and the relationship I knew would never be again.

"You know your sister and I don't get along." I told my best friend Teri when she picked me up to go out.

Ty and I returned three weeks ago and I hadn't heard from him since. He answers when I call but keeps telling me he's going through something and hangs up. I found out from Teri it's because C'Yani delivered a stillborn. It's unfortunate and regardless if I'm fucking her man or not, I wouldn't wish losing a child on anyone. And before anyone asks, no Teri doesn't know about me and Ty. She'd probably stop fucking with me.

It's not like we hooked up on purpose. It kinda just happened. He came to the club, got super drunk, had me perform a private show and from there we crossed the line. Shit, I'm glad I did because Ty has a hella lot to offer. He's got money, can fuck and suck me real good and gets me whatever I want. She may be his main chick but I'm still reaping the wifey privileges.

His girl and I were only cool through Teri so it's not like I stepped on her toes. From what he says, she's boring in bed and doesn't give him head. First off, he's dumb for telling me because you never discuss what goes on with wifey to your side chick. Second, of course I'm gonna fulfill each fantasy. I may have taken him from her but ain't no bitch taking him from me. Say what you want, but if he ain't with C'Yani, he ain't with no one. And no, I don't wonder if he's sleeping with her at home because like he said, she's boring so why would he bother?

"What's up with that?"

"I don't know. One day we were cool and the next we weren't." I told Teri on the way to pick her up. Her sister got off work late so we had to go back and get her.

"Yea well friend or not, don't start no shit. If you don't wanna speak to her; don't. And don't make no faces or talk shit."

"I won't damn. Relax." I pulled the visor down when she pulled up and blew the horn to fix my makeup. We were going to this new club some guy named Shak opened. I don't know his real name but it's what the streets called him. Evidently, he's the man out here and this is only one of the

44

businesses he had. Hell yea, I'm tryna meet him or a friend. Most ballers flock together and a bitch tryna get paid. Ty has money too but baller money is always better. I closed the visor and rolled my eyes when she stepped out.

The bitch had on a mid-length all black fitted dress. There was a split on the right side and it was strapless. She had a burgundy colored curly weave in that was fire. Whoever did her hair, hooked it up. She had on the new Giuseppe heels and a small clutch to match. I see why Ty kept her close. The bitch was bad by all means and I was silently hating.

"Ok sis. You killing the game." Teri joked when she closed the door.

"Hello." She spoke and I waved. I'm not ugly at all but when another gorgeous woman is with you, intimidation sets in quick whether we admit it or not. Every chick wants to be the baddest and when you step out with others you had to be on point.

"Ok Cee. I know this isn't your type of club but I had to get you out." Teri pulled off.

"What kind of club is it?" I turned and she was digging in her purse for something.

"Not uppity and has more minorities than anything." Her head popped up. I snickered because she'd rather be in a rock club some damn where.

"Teri you know I don't do hood or ghetto."

"I know but this spot is brand new and only ballers and people with money can get in." She sucked her teeth.

"We have money sis."

"I know and I'm not here for a man. I wanna dance and have a good time. I want my sister next to me too." She blew her a kiss in the rear view.

I admired their bond and wish I had one with my own family. My sister was two years older than me, married with kids and my brother is in the military and could care less. My mom and I never had a good relationship and my dad is always on her side. Teri is probably the closest person I have to being a sister.

"Ok. We're here." I noticed the line and smiled at all the fine niggas. Ty is my man but it never hurts to add to the equation.

"Ummmm." She was very hesitant to get out.

"No one is going to bother you. Look, we're getting valet and I have three tickets to bypass the line." She held them up.

"Tickets? You need tickets to get in?"

"Tonight you do because it's the grand opening and only certain people can attend. They have celebrities coming too so let's get it popping." Teri did a little dance in her seat as we waited in the valet line to pull up. I glanced around and there were Bentley's, Rolls Royce, Maserati and other hot whips. Shit, I'm definitely getting a side nigga tonight.

"Got damn he fine." Teri shouted and we all looked at the guy who just came out. He had a medium brown complexion, a ceaser haircut, it appears to be a nice build under the Tom Ford suit he wore and the glasses accentuated the outfit. He was definitely fine as fuck.

"Who is the guy next to him?" We both snapped our neck to look at C'Yani.

"What? I asked because some woman is yelling behind him and he's ignoring her." We turned and sure enough some chick was standing next to the guy with her arms folded. You could tell she had attitude and was talking shit. I knew exactly who he was and kept it to myself. I didn't know they knew one another.

"Let's go y'all." Teri let the valet dude open her door and another came over to me and did the same. C'Yani refused to wait and got out on her own. I heard men yelling *damn*, and *they bad*. My head was gassed up until we made it to the door. Both of the men were still standing there but neither paid me any mind.

"How are you ladies?" The one Teri laid eyes on first asked and kissed the top of her hand. Did she know him and didn't tell me?

"We're good. Here's our tickets." She handed them to him and he didn't let her hand go.

"Umm let go." C'Yani said and the two of them busted out laughing.

"My sister is very overprotective as you can see."

"And she should be with the way you look." Teri's face became flushed instantly.

"Tell the bouncer to place you in one of the VIP sections. I need to keep my eye on you." He bit down on his lip and my panties got moist. He was even sexier up close and when he did that, I was mad she saw him first. She laughed it off and we all stepped in.

The club was packed and nice as shit. It was three floors and VIP was at the top. He had 10 of them altogether and when you stepped inside, the damn floor had fish under the glass. It was weird as hell seeing them swimming below my feet.

The chairs were plush and the tables were lit up in lavender. The wrap around couch and two mini tables were nice too. The best part and C'Yani peeped it is, if you press the red light, the damn curtain closed off your section. There was a television and if you pressed a different button a bottle girl/ waitress came.

"This is very nice. And we're the first to sit on the couches." C'Yani smirked and pulled a price tag off.

"THREE THOUSAND DOLLARS FOR A COUCH." I didn't mean to shout. I heard about going all out for your house but money must not be an object for the owner if he doing it for his club.

"It's worth it." She plopped down and you could tell by her face she enjoyed the comfortable feeling.

"You good sis?" Teri asked and she nodded.

"Let's go dance." She took my hand and we went down to dance on the second level. There were sections to sit but nothing like VIP. The song Chun Li came on and you would've thought the two of us were Nicki. We knew people were watching and started being extra.

"I'm thirsty." Teri shouted after dancing. We had to be down there for a good hour or longer. The DJ played all the hot shit.

"Where's C?" We looked around and didn't see her anywhere.

"Oh my God Teri. You have to see the bathroom. I could poop in there and be comfortable." We busted out laughing.

"I'm serious. You can't hear this music." She waved her hand around the club.

"Its' quiet in there?"

"No, it's elevator music playing in there making it peaceful. There's two stalls and I think the doorknobs light up when you touch it." We stared at her.

"How much you drink?" She smiled.

"Only this many Ciroc's." She said two and held up five fingers. If my memory serves me right, she's never had a drink in her life.

"Press the button Jasmine. She needs water." I did like she asked and told them to bring up five waters.

"I know she won't drink them all but they'll be around." Teri said and a few minutes later a waitress stepped in our section and so did the guy at the door.

51

"Y'all good in here?" He questioned, bypassed me and went straight to where Teri was.

"She's never drank so I'm making sure she has water. Why are you here?"

"When someone asks for five waters at a time, it usually means someone's drunk as shit and tryna flush it out. Yo, go get her one of those pills." He shouted to the waitress.

"Hold up. My sister don't take pills." Teri had her hands on her hips.

"Calm down shorty. Ain't no rapist over here. I have my staff bringing her some Advil because most likely she'll have a hangover in the morning." The chick walked in with the packets and handed it to C'Yani.

"I'm fine." She attempted to stand and her ankle gave out. She screamed and when we looked the shit was definitely broke.

"Get Trey up here and make sure no one is on the elevator."

"Elevator?" I questioned with an attitude.

"We walked all those steps for nothing." Dude turned around, looked me up and down and shook his head.

"What?" Now my hands were on my hips.

"Aren't you a stripper?" Teri covered her mouth.

"Ex stripper and what does that have to do with anything?"

"You should be used to being on your feet."

"No, the fuck you didn't." I charged in his direction and stopped quick.

CLICK!

"First rule of thumb when around. Don't ever walk up on me." My hands went straight up.

"Take yo ass downstairs to meet them."

"Hell no. We all going..." He pressed the gun on my forehead harder and basically used it to push me out the section.

"Do I need to make an example outta you already?"

"It's ok sir. I'll go down with her. Can you make sure he brings my sister?" Teri had her hand on his arm.

"I can see you're gonna be a problem. I suggest you look me up before another word leaves your mouth to address me." He put the gun in his waist and looked Teri up and down. Only difference is, he smiled.

"You better not leave me with these strangers." Her sister cried out as the bouncer guy picked her up. She looked at me.

"I'll meet you downstairs."

"Are you kidding me?"

"Jasmine cut the shit. You know this isn't her type of vibe. I'll be right down."

"Again, she's gonna be a problem. Get her the fuck outta here." I felt someone grab my arm and almost drag me down the steps.

"I can walk." I snatched away and went to the stairway.

"I suggest you do it before I throw you down those same steps you're refusing to walk." He moved closer.

"I'm the nigga your mama warned you about. Take heed because I'll be the nightmare you never wake up from. Now get the fuck out my face." My heart was beating fast and

54

if I didn't hold it, I'd probably use the bathroom on myself. Whoever this man is, had me scared for my life and that never happens.

The security guy pointed outside and had me walk out. There was an ambulance waiting on the side of the building for C'Yani and I was shocked. What type of power does this nigga have? Scared or not, I need to find out and get closer. He could be my prince charming.

"You just gonna walk around this club and not say shit to me?" Kim barked behind me as I tried to ignore her. She's been annoying the shit outta me since she stalked me down in here. I threatened to leave and the bitch said she was gonna scream out I tried raping her in the bathroom and I didn't wanna bring attention to Shak's club. He worked hard opening his businesses and I'm not about to let her ruin it.

"Kim, you're not supposed to be anywhere near me. Why the fuck are you here anyway?" I stood in the corner to get away from the crowd. I made sure to stay in camera view in case she pulled some bullshit.

The night she had me arrested in my own house, I assumed the cameras I placed in there would catch everything she did. However, she must've disabled and took all my shit before she started with her suicide antics. I understand her not wanting to break up but if a man tells you it's over then move the fuck on. It's been two years and I haven't seen or heard from her. Why in the hell is she back?

"Come up here with me." Shak gestured his head for me to follow him into one of the VIP rooms.

"Stay here."

"Meek."

"Stay here and I'll be right back." Secretly I was praying someone started shooting and killed her dumb ass. I ain't shit but if you been through what I been through with her, you'd feel the same.

We stepped in one of the VIP areas and there were sexy ass women everywhere. Some were half dressed and others were falling over each other from being drunk. Shak gave me a look and I pointed to two of them. Hell yea, we about to go fuck. Not the ones overly intoxicated though. Ain't nobody tryna do time for bitches screaming out they were drugged. Hell, to the no. I got too much shit to lose.

"Meek." I turned around and Kim was standing there with her arms folded.

"Didn't I tell you to wait downstairs?" I pushed her out the section.

"You were taking too long."

57

"Kim you ain't my bitch. Take your ass the fuck home."

"I'm not leaving until you do."

"I'll see you at the spot." I told Shak and had security stay around him. I hated to leave him alone because it's not how we roll. Unfortunately, I had no choice but to get this delusional chick outta here.

I snatched her up by the arm and basically drug her down the steps and out the club. She tripped and almost fell when we got outside. I flagged down the valet dudes, asked for my rent a car and tossed her inside when they pulled up. Not only was I mad about taking her outta here, but I'm pissed because now she knew what car I had. I only drove it here because my new truck was getting rims put on it. I have insurance on the rent a car but who the fuck wants to deal with her messing up another vehicle?

"This shit has to stop Kim." I pulled into the road and drove off.

"Meek, I'm sorry about getting you arrested." I glance over at her and this bitch literally had her clothes off just that fast.

"Put your damn clothes on."

"You don't miss me baby?"

"HELL NO!" She hopped on top of me and I almost crashed.

"Yo!" I pulled over and she tried her hardest to get my jeans down. Thank goodness for belts because if these were sweats, I'd be done. She was kissing on my neck and I hate to say it, but my man was waking up. I had to think quick because if anyone stopped by its no telling what she'd say.

"Kim, sit over there and play with yourself."

"I want you to do it."

"I have to drive. You know I love to watch." It wasn't a lie. I enjoyed watching her get off and made her do it a lot.

"You better watch me."

"I am." She had her knees on the seat, her back arched against the glove compartment and her fingers twirling in her pussy and circling her clit.

"Meekkkkk, I miss having you inside me." I pressed record on my phone when she closed her eyes. I didn't have the video facing her but I damn sure wasn't about to take a charge if we got pulled over.

"How much do you miss it?"

"A lot. Mmmmm, I'm gonna cum already." Two minutes and a whole lotta moans later, her body shook and she came on her hands.

"Here you wanna taste?" Now any other time, I'd have no issues with it but not this time.

"Put your clothes on Kim." I handed them to her.

"Meek, why are you treating me this way?"

"Kim, you had me fucking arrested for beating on you and I didn't even touch you."

"I'm sorry about that. The police are easy to fool, aren't they? Beat yourself up, cry a little and BAM! They believe your entire story."

"What the hell is wrong with you?" Her arms were folded as she sat in the passenger seat pouting like a damn baby.

60

"I love you Meek and you're just throwing me away for some new bitches." I parked in front of her mother's house and stared. I don't know if this is where she's been staying, but its where I'm dropping her off at.

"Are you serious?"

"Yes I am."

"Get out." I stepped out my car, went to her side, took her out and threw all her clothes at her.

"You need help Kim and until you get it, we can no longer be cool." Not that we were but I had to say it. I don't know what the fuck ticks her off.

"Well take your stuff." She stormed in the house and left the door opened. I sent a text to Shak telling him it's still on. He told me to hurry up because those chicks were ready. He sent me a photo of them and I must say, I planned on having a good ass time tonight.

"You gonna disrespect me with those bitches?" Kim was over my shoulder looking in my phone. She had on a robe and not one single box in her hand or on the porch.

61

"Where's the stuff you claim to have?" I ignored her comment and placed my phone in my pocket.

"Fuck you Meek. I'm gonna burn it up." I shook my head and walked to the driver's side.

"Burn it. I can replace whatever it is."

"MEEEEEKKKKK!" She ran over and hugged me.

"Please don't leave." She tried putting her hands on my neck but I moved them.

"Bye Kim. Seek help." I sat in the car and was about to close my door.

"You're gonna need help." She shouted and I felt a pain in my side. I looked down and this crazy bitch stabbed me in the side with a damn steak knife or something. I almost went running after her, but in my head, I knew it was a trap. I closed the door with the knife still in my side and drove to the hospital. I text my cousin about taking a rain check because it ain't no telling how long I'll be here.

****

"What the hell happened to you?" Shak asked me the next day.

"Man, the bitch is crazy." I explained the shit she did and he too was aggravated.

"You can't have the bitch showing up everywhere you go." I ran my hand over my face as the nurse handed me my discharge papers.

They gave me five stitches and an antibiotic in case an infection set in. Evidently, the crazy bitch had something red on the knife. Because I had no clue what it was, I requested an AIDS test and any other STD or infection test I could. She is liable to do anything an I wasn't taking any chances.

"I'm trying not to kill her because I still got love for her but I don't know how much more I can take. What if I get a new woman? I can already tell she'll be going after her."

"Yea. You need a ride?" He asked walking me out the door.

"Nah, I'm good." I noticed him turn to go back inside.

"Where you going?"

"Shorty from last night still here." He hit me with the peace sign and jogged in the hospital. I shook my head at his crazy ass.

"What the hell?" I said to myself. There was a bouquet of flowers and a note on the windshield. I opened it.

My dear Meek. I love you to death. I turned the paper over to see if anything else was on it and it wasn't. I put it in my pocket, called my lawyer and had him meet me at my house. I sent him the recoding and gave him the letter. I'ma need all the proof I can get for when I murder her.

I stared at the man take control and make sure my sister was ok. He had the bouncer carry her out and an ambulance carted her off to the hospital. I thought about driving in the back but then how would Jasmine get home? I couldn't leave her like that.

I told C, I'd be right there and called my parents to tell them what happened. It was late but they always told us it didn't matter what time it was, if anything went down to contact them. My father said he'd meet me there shortly and my mother would come in the morning since my brother was asleep.

As I waited with Jasmine for valet to bring my car around, the guy came out with his friend who too was fine. It wasn't the same one from earlier though. I wonder where he went because C'Yani definitely asked about him when Jasmine wasn't paying attention.

The two of them spoke for a few minutes and made their way to us. I had to control my urge to jump on this man or even take him home; that's how fine he was. The way he took control and the amount of power he held, turned me on too. I loved an aggressive and ignorant man. I don't want him that way towards me but you get where I'm going.

"Give this to your sister." He handed me a card just as my car was brought around.

"You want me to have her call you?"

"This is the number to the insurance company for the club. If she files a claim for getting hurt they'll handle it. As far as her calling me, only if it's about that. You're the one who can call me for personal and pleasure." Jasmine sucked her teeth and sat in the car.

"This you?" He pointed to my brand-new Tesla. I loved this car.

"Yup. I just got it a week ago." He walked around it.

"How's it drive?"

"You have no idea. I find myself getting behind the wheel and jumping on the highway just because."

"That nice huh?"

"Very."

"Shak, how you out here with this bitch and we inside waiting for you." And there goes my infatuation. I should've known a man this fine would be taken.

"Bitch?" I tossed my purse and phone in the front seat. Jasmine noticed and stepped out too. She's definitely my ride or die chick.

"Go inside Barb."

"BARB?" Jasmine and I both laughed.

"What? You fucking bitches with their grandmother's name?" I asked and he thought it was hysterical.

"I got your grandmother."

"Bring it nana." He stepped in front of her just in time.

"Take her in." One of the security dudes escorted her back.

"So what's up shorty? You gonna call or what?" I sat in the car and he held the door opened.

"Not at all."

"Why not?"

"Ugh, your girl is one reason."

"She's not my chick but I am fucking her." He licked his lips and for a split second I thought about exchanging numbers but then my common sense kicked in.

"YO SHAK!" The security dude told him the girl was inside cutting up.

"Shak? Like the owner of this club?" I didn't even pay attention to his name when the girl said it the first time.

"That's me sexy. Can I get your number now?"

"You definitely can't have it now. Peace." I closed my door and pulled off.

I heard the rumors about him and needed to steer clear. Word is, him and his cousin run the streets and people are petrified of them. Not to mention dude supposedly has mad bitches and three of them stay in the same house as him. They on some sister wives type shit and I ain't down with it. He can be sexy all he wants but I draw the line with allowing my man to fuck whoever. It's the reason I'm single now.

Brian was the love of my life. I loved him with everything I had. We planned on getting married, having kids and living happily ever after. You know the fairytale life every chick wants. However; he was Caucasian and his family never approved of our relationship. His mom wasn't as bad as his father but it tore us apart because he was very family oriented.

They'd have events, dinners and he'd always ask me to come but it would end up with me cursing someone out. After a while, it took a toll us and I no longer wanted to deal with it. The breakup was hard on me and it got worse when I found out last year, he became engaged to a white woman. I knew it was to please his family but it still hurt. To this day, I can see him and walk right past without saying two words.

"He was fine Teri. You sure you're not gonna call him?"

"Positive. You heard the same shit I did so we both know it wouldn't work." She gave me the side eye. It's no secret she's had threesomes with women and the guy she's dealing with but that's not for me. I don't and won't share my man with anyone but my kids and I don't even want any at this point. I'm 24 and living my life to the fullest. A child would interfere and I don't have time. I dropped her off at home and drove to the hospital.

My dad called to see where I was because C wanted to make sure I didn't get hurt too. I loved my sister to death and would do anything for her. That's why if I knew who her man cheated with, I'd beat the bitch ass. C'Yani didn't know how to fight and the times I tried to teach her, she cried after I punched her in the stomach. I think it's why I'm overprotective of her. She's the same and would get her ass beat if necessary.

"They took her to get an MRI." My dad hugged me.

"Why that?"

"They said the X-ray is showing a break and they want to get a better look. What happened?"

"She was drinking."

"Drinking?" I put my hands up.

"I was on the dance floor and came up to find her like that. The owner offered her some Advil, she tried to stand and prove she was fine and fell."

"She's always been clumsy."

"Exactly daddy, which is why she should've never been drinking." He agreed and the two of us sat there for hours.

Evidently, her ankle was broken in two places and she needed emergency surgery. We were in for a long night.

****

My mom came up with my brother this morning and brought us something to eat. I felt my phone go off and checked my messages. The number wasn't stored so I had no idea who it was until I opened it up. How did this crazy nigga get my number?

Unknown: *License plates really give out a lotta info. You know I can stop by your house if I want?* I chuckled.

Me: *Go ahead. I'm not there.*

Unknown: *I know you're still at the hospital. The fall must've been bad.* I turned and this sexy ass man was leaning on the wall staring at me and here I am in the same thing from last night. He probably thinks I'm a dirty bitch.

He, however; had on a gray sweat suit and of course I looked down at the print. I couldn't see shit because the hoodie was too big. He was just as handsome now, as he was last night.

"Who is that honey?" I turned to tell her and she had the biggest grin on her face.

"Ma, I need to know why you grinning?"

"I may be white but when I see a fine black man, I'm going to say it."

"Claire get over here and leave them alone." My father barked and she listened. He loved my mom and it made me want the same kind of love they had. Twenty-two years of marriage, three kids and no cheating. I definitely wanted the same one day.

"Stalking doesn't become you."

"Women usually do the stalking sexy. I'm only here because my cousin got in some shit and needed a few stitches."

"Is he ok?"

"Nothing he can't handle."

"Why are you here with me then?" I tried to fix my clothes and hair but it was no use.

"You're better looking than him." I felt myself blushing and put my head down. He used the tip of his index finger to put it up.

"Have dinner with me."

"No thanks."

"Why not?"

"Look Shak. I'm not the kind of woman you're into." He folded his arms and stared down at me.

"What kind of women do I prefer since you know everything?"

"Ratchet, funny looking, has a built-up body, nappy ass weave and too much makeup. Plus, I don't do threesomes."

"Well damn, if you don't do those you're definitely not my type." My mouth dropped.

"What? I love watching women do each other. It gets my dick hard and once we all indulge, I can't even tell you how much fun it is."

"Goodbye." I attempted to leave and he grabbed my hand.

"I'm always gonna keep it a hundred with you but on some real shit, I wanna take you out." He intertwined his hand in mine and placed a kiss on my neck. I damn near fainted. It's been a very long time since I had sex. *A year, two days, thirty-*

two minutes and eighteen seconds to be exact. Any touch from a man would have me hot and bothered.

"I have to say no." He backed away and smirked.

"You holding that pussy hostage like I won't take it." I turned to see if anyone was paying attention because he was pretty loud.

"Will you stop being loud?" I whispered loud enough for him to hear.

"Not until you agree to a date."

"I said no."

"And I said, don't make me stop by your house and fuck you so good you'll wanna have a threesome with me."

"Will you stop with the sex shit?"

"Nope because whether you admit it or not, you're hot and bothered. You're thinking about how good this tongue will feel going up and down that pussy, or when my dick gets to…"

"Ok. Ok. One date." He kissed the back of my neck and told me to be ready Friday at eight. I watched him stroll down the hall and went to sit with my parents.

"Did they put C in a room yet?" My mom pulled me to the side.

"Teri, I don't usually get in your business but honey he is FINEEEEE! You need to give him some so you can stop being mean to everyone."

"MAAAAA!"

"What? When Brian supplied you, we never had an attitude from you. You've been really grouchy lately." She shrugged and went over to my dad. I looked down at my phone going off and it was him again.

Unknown: *Wear a short dress so I can finger pop you under the table.*" I sent him the middle finger and shut my phone off. Who the hell raised his ignorant ass and I hope he knows ain't no fucking going on.

"You ok?" I sat on the bench waiting on my mom to pick me up. I stayed in the hospital for four days because the pain was so bad, I kept falling back to sleep with the medication. The doctor said I broke two parts in my ankle. The tibia and talus and boy did it hurt. It was my first time drinking and I bet my last.

"Hello." I looked up to see the guy from the club. Not the one who was drooling over my sister but the other one. I looked him up and down and caught myself from being a stalker. This man was gorgeous and had I not appeared to be homeless, I may have spoken to him. My clothes were fine but I was alone and probably looked crazy.

He was brown skinned but not too dark, with dreads to the middle of his back. He had two humungous diamond earrings in his ear and the cap covered his eyes but the little I did see showed mystery. They were dark brown and I felt he could see straight through me.

The orange shirt showed the few tattoos on his arms and some on his neck. I'm shocked because most street dudes are covered in them these days. The Bentley truck he stepped out of played old school music which I appreciated. I cannot for the life of me get into the music they play on the radio today and turn my iPod on as soon as I'm in the car.

"I'm sorry. What did you ask?" He chuckled.

"I asked if you were ok?" He stood in front of me and I don't know why but I snapped.

"Yes, I'm ok and why are you standing there? How am I supposed to see my ride pull up if you're blocking my view?" His smile turned into a frown.

"Who the fuck you talking to like that?" He barked and I became nervous.

"Excuse me."

"Excuse me." He mocked and put his foot on the bench.

"I was tryna be nice to you but I can already tell you're one of those high sadity bitches."

"Bitch?" I was offended and grabbed my crutch. He removed it out my hand and threw it on the ground.

"That's right bitch. You talk in a white women's voice and by these raggedy ass clothes, I can tell you're stuck up." He popped the collar on my polo shirt. I happen to like these shirts from JC Penney. They're very comfortable.

"Don't touch me."

"You should be happy somebody wanna touch your corny ass." He mushed me in the head and walked off. *Did he just mush me?* Some dude was in the front seat rolling a joint, cracking up.

"Hey you?" He called out and I looked.

"What?" I snapped.

"Don't get smart with me bitch. I'm tryna help you out." I crossed my arms.

"How so?"

"First off, if I were you I'd fix my face because it makes you look a mess. Second, that's Meek and he's not the type of nigga you wanna talk shit to."

"Meek? What is a fucking Meek? Is that even his real name?" I was becoming so mad; curse words were rolling off my tongue.

"Ask around ma. From here on out be respectful and he won't do shit to you. Come out your face again and I can bet my money, he'll shoot your face off." He said calmly.

"Well he doesn't have to worry about me saying anything to him. I don't deal with thugs, hoodlums or ghetto men." I stood and started hopping to get my crutch he tossed. I should've stayed where I was.

"What the fuck you say?" I froze when he spoke. I didn't see him come out the hospital. Where did he come from?

"I... I... didn't say nothing."

"That's what I thought. Go get your crutch." He pushed me in the bushes and I could hear them laughing.

"Next time keep your mouth shut. Stupid ass bitch." I struggled getting up and when I did, I tossed my crutch at his truck.

"Got damn jerk."

SCREEEEEEECH! His brakes made a loud noise.

"Oh shit. Oh shit." I literally peed on myself when he backed up. I was so embarrassed, I fell back in the bushes just

79

so no one could see my wet pants. He stepped out and stood over top of me.

"You lucky, I don't put my hands on women, otherwise; I'd beat the shit outta you."

"Technically, pushing me in the bushes and mushing me in the head is the same but who cares, right?" I sat there staring at this handsome man terrorize the heck outta me and got turned on. What the hell is wrong with me?

"Be happy that's all I did. Do me a favor tho?" I sucked my teeth. He moved close to my ear.

"Take yo pissy ass home and wash. That pussy probably stinks and you're gonna have flies circulating this area soon." He took his index finger and mushed me again. I was so embarrassed, I sat there and started crying.

"C'Yani, what's wrong and why are you in the bushes?" My mom helped me up and stared at my clothes.

"Did you pee pee on yourself?" She said it like I was a child.

"Ma, really?"

"Don't get mad at me young lady. You're the one with wet clothes." She opened the door and told me to sit on her jacket because she refused to let me mess her seats up. Today has been the worse day ever. I was called a bitch three times, damn near attacked, embarrassed and used the bathroom on myself. What else could go wrong?

"Great!" I noticed Jasmine's car in the driveway and asked my mom to take me to her house. We may have hung out at the club but I still don't care for her. I sent a text to my sister and told her I'd be at our parents. I don't have time to argue with anyone.

****

"You ok in there C'Yani?" My father asked. It's been a week and I'm still at their house. My mom catered to me and it was closer to my job anyway.

"I'm ok daddy." I turned the tub on and grabbed the shower head off the hook. I made sure my foot was secure on the side because I stll had a boot on.

"Ok. Me and your mom are going to the store. I'll lock up."

81

"Ok." When I heard the car pull off, I turned the shower head on Jetstream and placed it on my clit. I imagined the guy Meek and found myself becoming more aroused. The thought of him touching me had my nub growing.

"Forget this." I dropped the shower head and circled my clit faster. His dreads, tongue, and muscles were invading my thoughts.

"Sssssss." The pressure was building and I couldn't wait to release.

"Yes Meek. Yes baby." I called out for him and seconds later, exploded. My breathing was rapid and suddenly the urge to release another one came and then another. How in the hell can the thought of a man make me cum so many times? I didn't care because my body was floating after each one. I closed my eyes getting ready to drift off to la la land.

"Sissy. I'm hungry." I heard my brother whining from outside the door.

"Ok. I'll be right there." I let the water out and grabbed the shower head again. I laughed at myself because my clit was super sensitive and I don't think I've ever cum that hard.

Tyrone and I had boring sex. It's not like I didn't want to change up, I was just scared. I'd watch pornos and women seem to be in pain having sex in different positions and I didn't want that. If he went down on me, I'd cum but then feel bad if he got up wiping his face. I never knew if he was ok with it because he never said. I guess it doesn't matter at this point. He found love elsewhere and she had to be sexing him better than me, otherwise; why else did he leave?

I gave him everything but money because his family was well off too. He had my heart, time, I catered to him, never cheated, and we had fun together. If sex is the reason he dipped out, why didn't he talk to me about it? Yea, he brought it up a few times but when we got in the bedroom he didn't make any attempts to try other things. Maybe I don't do it for him sexually. Whatever the case, it's over and the Meek guy can invade my thoughts any time if I can cum like that.

"C'Yaniiiiii." He continued whining.

"I'm putting my robe on. Wait a minute." I had to hurry up because my brother will say you took too long and try to fix his own food.

"About time."

"Boy be quiet." I popped him on the head and took my time going down the steps with these crutches. After he ate, we watched a movie in his room and once he fell asleep, I went in my old room and did the same. I must say, I slept like a baby.

"You ain't shit for that." Shak sat in the passenger side of the truck still laughing about me pushing shorty in the bushes a couple of weeks ago. He'd probably really get a kick outta her if I mentioned she was so scared, she peed on herself.

"Fuck that stuck up bitch."

"How you figure she stuck up because her cousin damn sure ain't."

"Did you hear how she spoke? Or the way she looked at the club? Everything about her screams high sadity." I took a pull off the blunt and passed it back.

"But you'd fuck her?"

"Oh hell yea. She's definitely sexy as fuck but just my luck she can't take dick." He almost choked.

"I'm serious. She's the type to want it one way and think being a freak is nasty and beneath her."

"It's probably because of her ex." I glanced at him and back at the road.

"Who is that?"

"Tyrone Simmons."

"Say word." He was corny too and tried to hang with street niggas and every time he did, someone always cursed him out or threatened to kill him.

I don't know why people think the streets is where it is because it's not. No one grows up wanting to do it but sometimes it's the cards you're dealt with. When corny people come around street dudes take offense because it's like you're making fun of them. Who rich in their right mind would hang in the streets? Exactly!

"Word."

"Yo, I thought he was fucking the stripper bitch."

"He is but that ain't the best part." We were at a red light so I gave him my full attention.

"Her and Teri best friends and she has no idea."

"No way."

"Yup. When Teri mentioned me pulling the gun on her I asked how they were affiliated. When she told me, I almost slipped up but caught myself. That ain't my shit and if she gets mad, then I'm not getting the pussy. They'll find out on their own."

"Damn. No wonder she was hating on her at the club."

The night we met them, I noticed how gorgeous C'Yani and her sister were. Jasmine was nice looking too but we knew she was a ho from being at the strip club. She allowed niggas to fuck if they paid her. I also paid attention to her facial expression when C'Yani stepped in front of her. She rolled her eyes and the jealousy was outta control. Yup, I got all that from looking at her. Women assumed men only paid attention to their ass and shit. Not this nigga. I monitored everything because chicks are as grimy as men.

I can't front, C'Yani is definitely the type of chick I'm looking to settle down with but she has a fucked-up attitude towards black men. It doesn't even matter that Tyrone is black. She wants those men who act the same as her. I'm not passive and have the ability to fuck her entire life up. Not in a bad way, but more of a stalking way. Shit, it's what I'm going through right now with my ex Kim. I was so in love with her, I wanted her to be next to me as much as possible and we see how that went. She is bat shit crazy and I can't seem to get away from her ass.

I may be an ignorant mothafucka, but when I love, I love hard and unfortunately, I fell for the wrong woman. Kim is worse than a stalker. Hell no I'm not scared but she's going to force me to kill her and I'm not tryna do time for her stupidity.

Like all women she thought her fucking me good would keep me, but again, I want a smart woman. Someone who initiates paying for things without expecting me to do it. Of course, I'll pay but the thought is all that matters. I appreciate having deep conversations with women because it shows their mentality.

My parents used to sit in the kitchen as I grew up and talk about everything, from the news to any issues they were having. I probably shouldn't have been listening but guess what? That communication kept them together up until my mom passed away five years ago. It's the reason I'm even in Jersey now.

She was coming home from work on a rainy day and was involved in a horrible accident on the highway. It was an eleven-car pileup and unfortunately, she didn't make it. After the services, my father wanted to be closer to our family so he packed up and said he was leaving California. It was too many memories and he couldn't handle being in the house without her. I wasn't gonna come but once he had my mother's body shipped back to Jersey so we can still visit her, I volunteered to accompany him.

I was in the process of starting my own construction company in Cali and changed everything here. It was tough starting but now my business is booming and money is no object. However; I do help my cousin out on the side. He's the boss, which is fine because the drug life ain't for me but when he needs shit handled, I'm right by his side.

We have younger cousins growing up who wanna be involved but Shak told them, they had to wait. I give it to him though, he's living his best life. Shit, he has a few bitches staying in the ho house he has and fucks on demand and others when he feels like it. Me, I can't get with that because no nigga will ever say he had my girl.

"I know but when shit hit the fan, I bet my ass say I didn't know." He slapped hands with me and stepped out at his house, or should I say mansion.

He would be stupid not to have a place of his own knowing those chicks fight on a regular. One thing I can say is, his mom taught him not to let a bitch at his home unless she's his main. Therefore; he won't have people showing up unannounced. I agree and had someone told me Kim was crazy, the bitch would've never been at my house.

"Same here. I'll hit you later."

"A'ight." He closed the door, I pulled out the driveway and headed to my own spot. I did make a detour to go and see my grandparents. My grandfather is a piece of work and my grandmother digs in his ass all the time. If I ever need a laugh, I'll call or stop by.

****

"Hey Meeky." My grandmother was outside water plants. Don't ask me why when its mid-July. She grabbed my cheeks like a little kid and planted a kiss on the right one.

"Grams, I told you to stop calling me that."

"Boy be quiet. Ain't no woman with you and you'll always be my Meeky." I waved her off and stepped in to see my pops and grandfather playing cards at the table with two other guys from the church. Oh, I forgot to mention my grandfather is a reverend. A perverted one but his congregation seems to love him.

"What up y'all?" I grabbed something to drink out the fridge, pulled up a chair and sat next to them.

"You hungry honey?" My grandmother washed her hands in the sink and went over to the stove where food was cooking.

"Always." She can cook her ass off so anytime she offered, hell yea I ate.

"Son, come over here and tell me if my hand is good." My pops couldn't play cards for shit but stayed in a game. I made my way over to him and stopped short when this bitch lifted her hand to knock on the door.

"What the fuck is this bitch doing here?" I didn't mean to be loud because my grandmother couldn't stand her. I walked out the kitchen, though the living room and stood at the door.

"Why is that crazy bitch on my porch?" I heard my grandmother shout behind me. It was a glass screen so Kim couldn't hear, nor did she care.

"Who?" I heard feet walking in my direction and then the screen unlocked in front of me. My grandfather, the reverend stepped out, placed the palm of his right hand on her forehead and started rebuking the devil outta her or some shit. Me, my pops and the other men were hysterical laughing.

"Take this crazy woman outta here Jesus. Lead her to a bar for a drink because she needs it." She was tryna pry his hands off but he was too strong. My grandma had to come out and pull him off.

"Somebody bring my holy water. This devil still standing here."

"What she needs is for me to beat her ass." My grandma went to swing and my pops caught her in time. Kim stood there popping shit so I snatched her dumb ass up, dragged her off the porch and pushed her to the ground. Oh, I may be a good man when it comes to my woman but don't mistake my kindness for weakness.

"Meek please talk to me."

"Bitch, you're not supposed to be within a hundred feet of me. You lucky I'm no snitch because I'd have yo ass locked the fuck up."

"Meek, I'm sorry for being crazy. If you take me back I'll be better." I felt a little bad for her but not much.

Shit, this bitch fucked up two of my trucks, damaged the windows in my house, told the cops I beat on her, had me arrested, and stabbed me in the side because I refused to be with her. It wasn't bad but my ass needed stitches.

"No can do." I walked to my truck and looked down at my phone vibrating. It was Shak asking me to pick him up and take him to Teri house.

"Meek please." I turned around and this crazy bitch was cutting her arms up with a razor. Blood was dripping and you could see the skin opening.

"What the fuck?"

"I'm gonna keep doing it until you take me back."

"I guess you'll be dead because we'll never be together again." I shook my head when she put it to her neck.

"What the hell?" My pops grabbed her wrists and held them apart.

"Call an ambulance." I blew my breath and dialed 911. I wanted no parts in this shit but as usual she put me in it.

"Why are you cutting yourself Kim?" My dad asked and my grandmother told him to let her die. She hated what Kim took me through and had no remorse.

"Please make him take me back."

"Kim they're other men out in the world."

"I ONLY WANT HIM. WHAT ABOUT OUR BABY?" All of them looked at her and I turned my face up. I knew she wasn't pregnant because we hadn't slept together.

"Boy, you about to have a demon child. Lord, I'm gonna need to baptize the kid ASAP because his mama is looney." My grandfather is funny as hell

"She ain't pregnant. Don't you know it's a ploy to keep me around? We haven't been together in a long time. The bitch is crazy."

WHOOP! WHOOP! Two cop cars and an ambulance pulled up at the same time.

"What's going on?"

"The bitch is crazy. I don't want her so she cut her arms up and threatening to off herself. She needs help." I hopped in my truck and pulled off. Her screams could be heard in the background but I'm over it and drove straight to my cousin's house.

I blew my horn at Shak's and lit a blunt while I waited. My life ain't in shambles, however; this crazy bitch is gonna be a problem. I can't be worried about being out and she pops up. What if she starts cutting her body parts again? I was shocked when she did it. Who knew she had issues like that?

"What up?" Shak closed the door and I began telling him what happened.

"Well damn. You're gonna have to get rid of her."

"I know. I'm just tryna find a way to do it. Anyway, why you not driving?" I passed him the blunt.

"Because when I'm ready to go she's gonna have to give me a ride."

"And?"

"And I'll fuck her right in the car." I busted out laughing and told him to give me her address. I loved my cousin to death but he is a damn fool.

"You coming in?"

"For?" He gave me the side eye.

"Nigga don't act like you ain't tryna see her sexy ass sister." I waved him off, took the keys out and made my way to the door with him. When we got there, you could hear arguing. Shak turned the doorknob and it was unlocked.

"Really nigga?"

"What? I have to make sure no one kills her before I get the pussy." He shrugged and went in.

"You like walking in peoples house unannounced?" The Teri chick came down the stairs in some fitted jeans, an off the shoulder shirt and sandals. She was just as pretty as her sister.

"Who the nigga yelling?"

"My sisters ex. She doesn't wanna be with him and he can't handle it." Shak turned to me.

"Don't look over here. She too high class for me." I put my hands up.

"Actually, she finds you very attractive." She walked around me.

"Yo, don't be giving my cousin the once over. We fucking, not y'all."

"We ain't doing shit nigga. You made me agree to one date and that's it. You better go fuck those birds in that ho house you running." I had to hold my stomach from laughing so hard. No other woman has dared to speak to him that way and he was lost.

"Anyway, you're too hood for her but I think you'd mesh well together." Shak yanked her by the hair and forcefully kissed her.

"Shak, you on some other shit. I'm out." Neither of them stopped so I guess she's cool with it.

"JUST GO TY! WHEN I NEEDED YOU SOME OTHER WOMAN HAD YOUR ATTENTION." Her sister yelled and we all stood there watching him stand at the bedroom door.

"I said, I was sorry."

"Sorry my behind." I snickered at her proper ness.

"FINE! CALL ME WHEN YOU LEARN HOW TO PLEASE ME." Teri turned her face up. I heard stomping and glanced up to see a boot on her foot.

"So you cheat because I didn't please you? Why didn't you just leave?"

"You have good pussy. You just have to learn how to fuck." I saw her look at him and then at us. I don't think she expected anyone to be listening but it was hard when they were loud.

"I'm gonna go."

"Who the hell is he C'Yani? He's here for you?" Once our eyes met, embarrassment was written all over her face.

"Nah bro. I'm dropping my cousin off. Peace." I said my goodbye to Teri and my cousin and looked up to see C'Yani wiping her eyes. I shook my head and left. What kind of nigga tells his woman she can't fuck and it's the reason he cheated? I'm telling you communication is key in a relationship. I hopped in my truck and drove home. I had enough shit going on in my life.

After my shower, I laid in my bed and checked the text Shak sent me. He claimed the guy disrespected C'Yani a little more and left. If she let him then it's exactly what she gets.

My phone started ringing just as I went to put it down. I didn't know the number and answered anyway.

"What?"

"Hi. This is the hospital contacting you about your fiancé Kim..." I cut her off.

"That bitch ain't my fiancé and how you get this number?"

"I'm sorry sir but she gave it to us. She has you down as her emergency contact."

"Do me a favor and take my name off any of her paperwork. I have a restraining order against her and she's not supposed to be anywhere around me. Therefore; I won't be picking her up, having no interventions; nothing. Peace." I disconnected the call and tossed my phone on the night stand. *This bitch is gonna make me kill her.*

"I think you should go Shak. We can do this another time." Teri said and opened the front door. The guy left about five minutes ago and I'm sure she wanted to check on her sister. I stayed on the bar stool continuing to drink my soda.

"Shak, my sister needs me and..."

"Ok, so go see her." She sucked her teeth.

I stood, grabbed her hand and both of us went in the room. Her sister was upset and wiping her eyes. I understand because dude played her the fuck out. I walked around the room and noticed the degrees, marketing books and other shit. You could tell she was smart but not smart enough to know the nigga fucking the other chick.

"Where your room at yo?" I was tired of standing there listening to the why's and what if's.

"Down the hall on the right." I went in her room and it was all black. I chuckled because usually men had rooms like this. The bed was huge and so is the television hanging on her wall. I can't front; shorty had a nice ass house and the decor was on point too. I took my shoes and clothes off and hopped in the bed.

"What you doing?" Teri's arms were folded as her sexy ass leaned on the door.

"Since you cancelled the date, I may as well stay the night."

"You bugging. Bye Shak."

"Ain't nobody bugging but you."

"What?"

"I already took my clothes off, which means I'm in for the night. Too bad. Now hurry up and get in here with me. I wanna feel your body next to mine."

"You got me fucked up." She had the nerve to say with an attitude. I moved the covers off and smirk when she bit her lip after realizing what I held in my boxers. I'ma decent size and I know how to fuck so she's getting a treat.

"I don't have shit fucked up but you do. Thinking you're gonna come in here demanding shit. Take these clothes off and hop in bed." We stared at each other for a good five seconds before I moved over to where she stood, and leaned in to kiss her. Our tongues were no match for each other because we both wanted to be in control. She hopped in my arms and I carried her over to the bed.

"I didn't expect to fuck but it's whatever you want." I lifted her shirt, unsnapped the bra and began sucking on her juicy ass titties. I could tell her body was yearning for me by the way her lower half grinded underneath. I removed her jeans and panties and smiled.

"You sexy as hell Teri." Her clit had already started to protrude outta it's lid. I spread her legs open and let my tongue slide up and down her folds.

"Teri can you help me?" Her sister yelled from outside the door. She sat up and looked at me.

"I'm coming."

"What?" I was aggravated.

"It's a sign we shouldn't be doing this anyway."

"Fuck a sign Teri." I moved on top and her legs wrapped around my back. I didn't even care about foreplay at the moment and slid my boxers down.

"You like this?" I let the tip touch her clit and she began arching her back.

"You got condoms ma?" I slid the tip in a little and pulled back out.

"Nooooo. Make me cum Shak." I think my man got harder hearing her moan. I slid the tip in again.

"Teri!"

"FUCK!!!!" She slammed her arms down on the bed.

"It's definitely a sign. We don't have no condoms and I probably would've put a baby in you."

"Move. I'm coming C'Yani." She tried to scoot off but I let my hand grip her pussy.

"I wanna see you cum."

"When I come backkkkkkkk. Oh shitttttt." My thumb circled her treasure as she fucked two of my fingers. I let my hand go behind her head and began kissing her.

"You're there Teri. Let it go." She nodded, bit down on my neck and came hard as hell.

"Now go see what your blocking ass sister wants." She didn't move for a few minutes and when she did, I had to help.

Once she stepped out I handled myself. It's been a long time since I've had to jerk off but my dick was hard, we can't fuck because there's no condoms and I had to release too.

I cleaned my hands and hopped back in the bed. I can't even tell you when she returned because I fell asleep. I do know when my eyes opened, she was directly under me. I kissed her cheek, got dressed and took an Uber home to change. I had things to do.

****

"Hey son. When did you get here?" My mom Tionne asked bringing in groceries.

"Just now. I was talking to Shawn about some stuff." I went out to grab the other bags.

If you haven't figured it out, my name is Shakim and I'm the sexy ass little cousin from Tina J's book, A Dope Boys Seduction. Fazza and Mazza are my cousins and no they still don't associate themselves with my mother. I mean they see each other at family functions and things like that but none of them speak.

I understand because even as a kid, I felt my mother not disclosing the information on who murdered my pops was wrong. And to this day, I still feel some kind of way about it but she's still my mother.

If you're wondering how Meek is related to us, let me break it down. My great uncle, is the nasty ass reverend. However, he had two sons. One named Mark and the other James. Mark still lives in New York with his family and James, is in Jersey.

Meek is James son, and my uncle is his grandfather. He and I always been close regardless of where he lived. Once he moved back five years ago, the two of us became tighter and have the streets on lock. Well I do because he doesn't dibble in the drug game but whatever I need, he's right there.

"I miss seeing you."

"Ma, don't tell him that because then he'll come over more." My sister Shakima yelled coming down the steps.

"I bet yo broke ass don't get no more money." My sister was younger than me and finishing her last year in college.

We both had money in the bank from our father but for some reason she couldn't touch hers until she was twenty-four, so guess who had to give her money? Yup! Me, my mom and our stepdad Shawn.

He adopted us a year after they married. Besides Shakima, I have two little brothers and another sister who can get whatever they want from me too. I don't call him pops but I do give him mad respect. Shit, my mom pushed out three kids for him too.

"Yes I will because I'll tell everyone you let your family starve." She gave me the finger and I put her in the headlock.

"Stop before you mess my hair up." I let her go and rubbed it.

"Shakim let me talk to you." Shawn said after I brought in the rest of the bags.

"Daddy tell him to leave your favorite alone." I sucked my teeth. Shakima called him dad and he loved it. He isn't and has never tried to take my father's place but my sister wanted that daddy's love and he gave it to her.

"You know good and well me and Shawna are his favorite." My mom shook her head because she knew I was right. Shakima might be the first daughter but Shawna has her beat. I have never seen a five-year-old more spoiled then her.

"Move." I mushed her in the head and stepped outside. "What up?"

"I just wanted to tell you how proud I am of you."

"Huh?" I was confused because he never gets sentimental with me.

"You suffered a tragedy when your father died and even though you were young, you witnessed a lot. I know you're out in the streets doing crazy shit but you're smart with it. You invested, have businesses, and take care of your siblings."

"You're not about to tell me you dying, are you?" He laughed.

"Not at all. I just wanna make sure if anything did ever happen to me, you'd take care of your mother and all the kids." I knew exactly what he meant.

"It doesn't matter if my sisters and brothers didn't come from my biological father. They're still my blood, even if they had a different mother I'd make sure they were straight. And if anything, ever happened to me I know you'd be here for them."

"Nothing will happen to you because even though you're in Jersey, I have men on the force looking out for you."

"What?" I wasn't upset.

"You're my son and I will not lose you to the streets or a hating ass nigga." He gave me a hug and so did my mom.

"I walk the straight and narrow as much as possible. I may not say it but I appreciate everything you do for us."

"Daddy, Shawna in here throwing stuff." My little brother Shawn said and ran over to hug me. Like I said, I will do anything for my family and them not having the same father means nothing. We share the same mother and Shawn has been here ever since. They are my blood.

"I'm coming. Remember what I said Shakim." I nodded.

"You staying for dinner?"

"Why not?" I ended up staying the night and I realized my family is the shit. We may not see one another a lot but our bond is still strong as hell.

Coming out the bedroom to yell at Ty is one thing but seeing that sexy thug dude standing there is another. I was embarrassed as hell when my ex shouted out I couldn't please him. Not that I'd consider giving the Meek guy any because I'm fine fantasizing over him but it's the point. He'd probably break me in two anyway. Thinking about Ty and his antics the other night pissed me off.

"You got men coming to see you now?" We were back in my room because I no longer wanted an audience. Teri and her friend walked into another room but I'm sure they could still hear.

"Ty, you heard him say he's not here for me. Don't try and put someone on me to cover up what you've been doing. And why does it matter?" He came closer and ran his hand down my face.

"I messed up really bad C'Yani."

"Yea you did." I wiped my eyes.

"Can we start over? I mean let's try and get back to where we used to be."

111

"Why would you be with a woman who can't sexually satisfy you?"

"I should've spoken to you about it more instead of dipping out and I'm sorry. I don't love the chick and if you take me back I promise to never see her again."

"I don't know Ty. You were messing with the woman for a year. Even I know feelings are involved."

"I care about her baby but I'll never love any woman the way I love you." He planted a gentle kiss on my lips and my body began to react. I wrapped my arms around his neck and he squeezed my butt.

"Mmmm. Let's go slow." I pushed him away.

"I'll do whatever you want just don't leave." He pecked my lips and went to the bedroom door.

"I'm sorry we lost our son but we can work on having another one." I gave him half a smile and plopped on my bed.

After he left, I went to speak to Teri but once I noticed the door closed, I refused to barge in. The guy was probably in there and I did not want to see any naked body parts by accident. Instead I returned to my room and waited for my

sister to come see what I wanted.

"You ok sis?" Teri came and rubbed my back.

"Is the guy still here? Is that why the door is closed?"

"Yea."

"You slept with him?"

"I promised him a date and after tonight, we're done."

I laughed.

"He ain't done until he sample's that coochie you

holding hostage. Isn't that what he told you at the hospital?"

Teri rolled her eyes.

"I'll see you later."

"Are you gonna free your coochie for him?" I

whispered.

"I may have if he didn't have hella ho's." I nodded and

told her I'd see her in the morning.

****

It's been a few days since the incident with Ty and he's

been calling me nonstop. I don't answer and when I do, I tell

him I'm busy. I'm not sure we could ever be together again

113

and leading him on is only going to make things worse, so I blocked him this morning and went for a drive to my favorite place. It was late but I wanted to see him and no one is out here anyway.

I parked in front of his spot, grabbed the teddy bear and stepped out. It was late but I had to come. It's been a few days and regardless of the time, it's where I should be.

Tyrone Simmons Junior is what the tombstone read. It's been two months since I lost him and it never gets easier seeing this monument. I pushed the leaves out the way, sat the bear down and started singing a lullaby to him. Every time I did it, the wind would blow a certain way. In my mind he was letting me know he heard. Call me crazy if you want but if anyone experienced this they're probably doing the same.

I sat there for a half hour thinking about how he would look. Would he be spoiled and all the other things he should've been doing had he made it. I turned my body to leave when it sounded like someone was coming. Footsteps are loud as hell when you're alone.

"Who's there?" I took the mace out my pocket and stood. The steps were getting closer.

"You better stay away or I'll shoot." The footsteps stopped for a few seconds and started up again. My heart was beating fast and I had the urge to run but with a boot on where in the hell am I going? I stood there and the minute I felt a close presence; began spraying.

"Awww shit bitch. Are you crazy?" I continued spraying and rushed to my car only to realize my keys were at the grave.

"Stay back or I'll spray again." The person snatched my wrist and forced me to drop the mace.

"What the fuck is wrong with you?" I turned around to see the sexy thug who left my place a few days ago wiping his eyes.

"Oh my God. I'm so sorry. I thought you were a killer." I hit the alarm and snatched the water bottle out the cup holder.

"Ain't no mace killing a killer." He barked.

"Here let me pour this in your eyes." He stopped wiping and allowed me to do it. I popped the trunk, grabbed two more bottles and did the same. I always kept a case in my car.

"Here you go." I took my jacket off and let him use the sleeve to wipe his eyes. I guess mace really works. After another ten minutes of getting himself together he looked at me. His eyes were blood shot red.

"Why are you out here this late?"

"Why are you? Are you following me?" I asked with my hands on my hips.

"Don't flatter yourself shorty. My mom is over there." He pointed to a different area.

"I'm sorry to hear that."

"Yea. They say she went fast and didn't feel a thing. I think it's why I'm not as devastated." I gave him a weird look.

"I'm hurt don't get me wrong but I know she didn't suffer or feel pain."

"Oh."

"Who are you visiting?"

"My son."

"Oh shit. My bad. I saw you over here and..."

"No, it's ok. I shouldn't be here this late anyway but I wanted to see him." He glanced at the name.

"The guy at your house is his father?"

"Unfortunately."

"If you don't mind me asking. What happened?" I blew my breath in the air to try and stop the tears threatening to fall. I don't know this man and didn't want him to see me cry.

"Long story short, Ty cheated on me and I continuously stressed myself out. I became depressed, wouldn't eat like I was supposed to and basically worked myself to death just to keep it in denial. The week before I lost him, I had a good doctor's appointment. I heard my son's heartbeat and couldn't wait to deliver. Unfortunately, exactly four days later, Ty goes away on a business trip with his side chick and I go into labor. I called him over and over and he wouldn't answer." I felt the tears rolling down my face. He had a sad look on his.

"I wanted him there and he refused to answer. I delivered my son only to find out he was already dead in my stomach. So, while my so-called fiancé was living it up, my parents had to bury our child because I couldn't do it." I felt myself shaking,

"I needed him and he was nowhere to be found. Why didn't he answer the phone? Why? Did he hate me that much? He should've just answered." I was hysterical by now.

"I don't know why he didn't answer ma." He put his arms around me and it's like I was safe. No one could hurt me at this moment.

After a few minutes of silence, I moved away.

"I'm sorry." I went in my glove compartment and grabbed some tissue. I wiped my tears and snot off his shirt and then used another piece for my eyes.

"Hold up." I looked at him.

"You had tissue and made me use your jacket sleeve to wipe my eyes." I started laughing hard.

"You ain't shit for that."

"I'm sorry. At the time I wasn't thinking and..." He lifted my face and stared.

"I don't know your situation and if what you're saying is true, then he's a foul ass nigga. However; what happened to you happens to a lotta women. It's God's way of telling you it wasn't time."

"You go to church?" He chuckled.

"My grandfather is a pastor and I try and make as many Sundays as possible."

"Oh."

"You're young C'Yani and there are other men who would treat you better."

"Would you?" No clue why I asked him but I'm curious to hear his answer.

"Any woman I've been with has always been treated with the upmost respect. But you. You're not ready for a man like me."

"A man like you?"

"I'm not a safe nigga C'Yani. I have a lot of rude and aggressive ways about me."

"You don't have to tell me. I saw it firsthand." He laughed.

"I'm serious. I'll wine and dine you and then make love to your mind, body and soul. Don't let this street image fool you. I know how to love a woman but you're into appearances and what people would say seeing you with a street dude. I want my woman secure and walking with her head held high at all times; giving the haters something to gossip about." I moved in between his legs, wrapped my arms around his neck, stood on my tippy toes with my good foot and used my tongue to ignite a fire I'm not sure I can handle.

He lifted me up, turned me around and sat me on the hood of my car. Both of his hands were on my face as we began kissing again; this time more passionately. It's like we were both trying to prove a point without words. I allowed my hands to slide under his shirt and felt his muscles. He must've noticed how nervous I was and stopped.

"You're beautiful C'Yani and a blind man can see that. You're just not ready for someone like me." He helped me down and walked me to the driver's side of my car.

"How do you know?" I caught an attitude.

"Watch." He unbuckled my jeans, slid them down to my hips along with my panties and let his fingers roam up and down the folds of my lower half. What in the hell am I doing allowing this man to touch me inappropriately?

He crashed his lips on mine and began circling my nub way better than me. I couldn't believe he was touching me in this way. I had been daydreaming for weeks and finally had the real thing.

"Let it go ma." I had a grip on his neck and my legs were shaking uncontrollably.

"Meek what are you?" He stuck two fingers inside, continued flickering my clit with his thumb and a minute later I felt blood rushing through my body as the current hit.

"Oh my gawddd. It felt so good." My nub was still pumping and I needed another one. I placed my hand on top of his and he started again.

"You sexy as hell." He let me finish, placed a few kisses on my neck and caught me from falling.

"This is nothing C'Yani. Imagine if I were inside you." He pulled my clothes up, sucked my juices off his fingers and sat me in my car.

"When you're ready for a real man to show you the ropes in the bedroom, call me." He pecked my lips and watched as I pulled off. Oh, I'm gonna sleep like a got damn baby tonight. I drove straight home, took a fast shower and went to bed. His fingers definitely did my body good.

What are you doing bro? I asked myself after watching C'Yani pull off. Not only is she broken from an unfaithful nigga; she lost a child. To make matters worse, I had her moaning my name and cumming all over my hand at the damn cemetery. My mom is probably rolling over in her grave seeing me do that. Being spontaneous is fun but I gotta do better.

I laughed thinking about her macing me and then couldn't help but feel bad for the tragedy she dealt with. She's is definitely strong if her ass can get up and go to work and not fall into more depression.

I'm shocked we ran into one another out there. I went to speak to my mom and even though she can't respond; it still felt good venting to someone. I thought about talking to my pops but he's at a loss for words as to why Kim bugging. She is really on some fatal attraction, thin line between Love and hate type shit. I could see if I were still sleeping with her but it's not the case. I'm smart enough to know if I did it would cause more harm than good. Had I known she'd do this anyway I should've.

123

I picked my phone up and called up shorty I've been hitting off as of lately. C'Yani had my dick hard as hell thinking about her lately and the pressure built up needed to be released. Once shorty confirmed she was on her way, I hopped in the shower and met at the hotel. Yea, no chick will at my house either.

"Two weeks is too long daddy. I need this a lot more." She said when I walked in the room. I can hold out on sex but like I said C, had me gone.

"Do your thing." I dropped the box of condoms on the table and let her go down to get the first nut out. When she did, we had a long night. The crazy thing is, I had C'Yani in my head a few times telling me to leave and wait for her. I pushed those thoughts to the side and bust a few more nuts

I may wait now to see where she and I end up but I had to get those out. I left shorty asleep in the bed and went home. I never stay the night because women think other shit and ain't nobody got time for that.

****

"Mr. Gibson, someone's here to see you." My secretary said with an attitude when she came in my office. I like to be in the field working but twice a week I stayed in the office to check over finances, contacts and other important stuff.

"Tha fuck wrong with you?"

"Nothing."

"Then why you say it like that?"

"No reason." She opened the door and told the person to come in. I had my head down looking at something when I heard her voice.

"Hello." I admit she put a smile on my face. It's been a couple of weeks since we've graced each other's presence and she did cross my mind quite a bit. I left her alone because she needed to heal from the guy and her son's death.

"Ummm. I didn't mean to upset her." I stared at her limp towards me with a brown bag. The boot was off but I guess her ankle is still healing.

"She a'ight. What's this?" I removed the bag from her hand.

"Well I wanted to thank you for letting me vent and..."

125

"And cum. I bet you slept good that night." Her face was flushed. I put a French fry in my mouth and pulled the burger out.

"What? You vented and I made you cum."

"Do you have to be so blunt?" I had to snicker at her innocence. I think it's what's drawing me to her.

"You're welcome."

"Like I was saying before you rudely interrupted me. I appreciate it and I'm sorry you had to hear the disrespectful things my ex said." I took a bite of my burger, wiped my hands with a napkin and stood next to her.

"Don't apologize for his ignorance."

"I shouldn't but..."

"But nothing. A real man wouldn't disclose that information out loud."

"He didn't know anyone was there." I turned her face to me because she started staring out the window.

"He may not have known my cousin and I were but he knew your sister was. And what if y'all friend came by?"

126

"I don't have any friends. Well, I'm cool with my secretary but that's it. If you're speaking of Jasmine she's my sisters' friend."

"Why don't you have friends?" She shrugged.

"Most African American women take one look at me, hear how I speak and write me off. They consider me to be stuck up and high class. I'm down to earth Meek." I started laughing.

"What?"

"You're down to earth in your own way and do you ever think women believe you are because of the way you portray yourself?"

"What you mean?" I sat back down to eat and offered her a seat across from me.

"You dress nice, you have a high position at your job and I can bet you never go out with people you work with. You hide out in the office and make up excuses on why you can't go. I can go on but you get it." I rolled my chair to the mini fridge and grabbed a water.

"I try to be nice to everyone and I don't hang with them because..." She stopped and laid her head back.

"I don't even know why." I went over and sat on my desk in front of her.

"Can you fuck?" Her head lifted up.

"Huh?"

"You heard me. Can you please me in bed if I took it there with you?" She was flustered and began fidgeting with her hands.

"Another reason why you're not ready."

"I didn't say anything." I went to lock my door.

"You don't have to. The way your fidgeting and getting nervous tells me everything I need to know." I leaned down and removed her shoes. She had some pretty ass feet.

"What are you doing?" I lifted her out the chair, unbuttoned the blouse, slid it off her shoulders and tossed it on the desk.

"People will come in and..." I pecked her lips.

"No one is coming in here and I'll turn the television up." I reached for the remote and raised the volume. It's not unlikely for me to do it. I had tons of people who came in and we watched the news or something.

I used my hands to unhook her bra and the way her breasts sat up made my mouth water. I got to her pants and she took them off on her own. Her thong panties were the only piece of clothing she wore. I stared at her take her time sliding then down her leg. Her pussy was shaved and her nipples began to harden.

"You ready ma?" I took my shirt off and undid my jeans. I could see how petrified she was.

"I'm nervous."

"Don't be. I won't hurt you." I picked her up with my pants almost falling and laid her sexy body on the desk.

"Ummmm."

"Relax C." She nodded and I let her stay in the position until her legs began to fall on the side. It showed me how relaxed she was. I spread them open, licked my lips and let my tongue roam in between her lips.

"Ssssss." Her back was now arched and her hands were on the top of my head.

"Oh my gawdddddd." She moaned out when I took over and ate her pussy.

"It feels so good Meek. Yessssss." She allowed me to taste her nectar and a nigga was hooked. I didn't stop and made sure her body received more pleasure than she's ever known. After the fourth one ripped through her, I was about to place my mouth on hers.

"Are you ok?"

"What you mean?"

"Did I cum too much for you? I didn't mean to." I shook my head grinning. This nigga couldn't have been fucking her right.

"If you didn't, I'd be questioning my skills and you taste real good." I placed my lips on hers and let my jeans and boxers go down to my ankles. My dick was so hard it would probably break if she touched it.

"You ready?" She nodded.

"I don't have any condoms but I promise to pull out." I didn't wanna have unprotected sex but it's too late. I ran the tip up and down.

"You sure you're ready?" She nodded yes again and I let the tip slide in slow. Her entire body tensed up. She used her elbows to sit up and looked down.

"That's not gonna fit in me." She pushed me off, got off the desk and quickly put her clothes on.

"Yo! I know you're not about to leave." I was fuming and angrier with my own self for allowing me to get this far knowing she'd most likely back out.

"I'm sorry Meek but I'm scared and you're way too big. My coochie can't handle that. It's going to hurt and..." She looked like she was gonna cry.

"Come here." I walked to her and slipped my tongue in her mouth. I was stroking the shit outta my dick. I refused to have blue balls and if kissing her is gonna make me nut, you damn right I'm doing it.

"Shit." I came in my hand and went in the bathroom to clean up. I didn't expect to see her when I stepped out because she's scared as hell. My secretary however; stood there looking upset.

"What up?" Nothing was outta place and you couldn't tell what we did.

"Did you sleep with her?"

"No, I didn't. She brought me lunch. Anything else?" She stood there with an attitude.

"You got one more time to question me about who enters this office or approach me with an attitude. The shit is aggravating and you'll be in the unemployment line soon." I told Mia, who is Kim's sister. She's worked for me since the beginning and always kept her nose in everyone's business. I never had a problem but then again, a gorgeous woman has never brought me lunch here. Now that I think of it, how did she find out where I worked?

"I apologize. It won't happen again." I plopped down in my chair. It's gonna take me a while but C'Yani will feel the effects of Meek soon enough.

"TERI!! TERI!!!!" I heard my sister shout and ran out the bedroom in my nightgown. I was off today and stayed in bed. She appeared to be disheveled and flustered. I know that nigga Ty didn't bother her.

"What's wrong? You ok?"

"I couldn't do it."

"Do what?" She was so frantic, she had me thinking she tried to kill someone.

"I couldn't sleep with him."

"Sleep with who?" She was speaking in circles.

"Meek."

"MEEK! How did that happen?" I had her sit on the couch and tell me.

"Ok so I brought him lunch and thanked him for letting me vent."

"And making you cum." I cut her off. When she told me about him doing that I asked her why didn't she let him fuck and she shrugged her shoulders.

"Anyway. He asked if I could satisfy him if he took it there with me. I didn't answer so he locked the office door, stripped me out my clothes and gave me the best head I've ever received. I mean he made me cum so many times."

"Really?"

"Yes, but the plot thickens." My sister is so corny. Who says the plot thickens?

"He kissed me and I asked if I came to much."

"If you didn't then it would've been a problem and what I tell you about that? A man wants to make a woman cum a lot. It shows he's doing a good job and most likely kiss right after."

"Right it's exactly what happened. Sis, he put the tip in and I tensed up." I smiled because I was excited to hear she let another man touch her in a sexual way.

"I stopped him."

"WHAT?"

"He was too big Teri. All of that wouldn't fit in me."

"Please tell me you didn't say that."

"I told him it wouldn't fit in my coochie."

"Oh my God, no you didn't." I was embarrassed for her.

"Sis, he kissed me and made himself cum in his hand. I ran out before he came from the bathroom. I'm so embarrassed." I busted out laughing so hard, she got mad and left me downstairs.

After I finished laughing, I went to her room and she was in the shower. I sat on the bed and her phone went off. The number wasn't stored so I put her passcode in and looked. I had to cover my mouth at what the message said.

Unknown: *I told you, you weren't ready. That pussy taste real good tho and trust we'll meet up again and I'm gonna take that body to ecstasy. You need to know what a real man feels like. Keep that pussy tight until next time.* I went in the bathroom and sat on the toilet seat.

"You did something right sis because he wants more."

"Why you say that?" She pulled the shower curtain back and listened to me read the message. She closed it back without saying anything so I responded for her.

C'Yani: *I can't wait. Your tongue feels so damn good, I can't imagine what the dick like.*

135

"Don't text him back." She shouted after looking at me.

Unknown: *Nice try Teri.*

C'Yani: *How you know it's me?*

Unknown: *We both know the word dick is too much for her to say and she doesn't speak like that but she will. Tell her, I got her when the time is right.* I repeated the message, listened to her shout OMG and went in my room.

"She good?" Shak asked and lifted the covers for me to get under. He's been staying the night and refuses to leave. The night we were supposed to go out, I asked him to leave and stayed home. Of course, he went nowhere and we almost had sex but C'Yani kept knocking on the door.

She ended up going to the cemetery a few days later and ran into Meek. Shak on the other hand has been here every night since then. It didn't matter if it was four in the morning and I had to work the next day, he still stopped by and left when I did. This man brought a toothbrush, pajamas and clothes for when he stayed.

"She's fine. Meek about to turn her out."

136

"I told that nigga she's the one for him. He keeps telling me he don't wanna be bothered."

"Yea well. He's bothered alright." He leaned down and kissed my lips. This is the most we've done since the first time.

"When you gonna turn me out?" He was on top using his elbows to keep his weight off.

"When you shut down your whore house, take an STD test and make me believe it's only me."

"Damn that's a lot."

"I'm worth it."

"You are and I promise to give it to you; eventually."

"Eventually? Get your heavy ass up." I wasn't pressuring him to do anything but I knew my worth and reused to settle.

"Nope."

"Come on Shak you're heavy."

"My weight ain't even on you." He wasn't lying. I wanted him up because his dick was touching my pelvis and I'm horny. He swiftly lifted my shirt and started massaging and sucking on my breasts. I wanted to fight him but I couldn't.

137

"Sssss." My hand was on his head and my body was on fire and he knew it. He placed kisses on my stomach and the minute his mouth touched my pussy, I jumped up. Hell yea I wanted it but it's not our time.

"Teri, I'm going out to eat. You coming?" C shouted behind the door. She knew he was here all the time and never walked in unless invited.

"Go head babe. I got stuff to do." He kissed me and stood to take a shower.

"I'm gonna give you what you want Teri because you're right. You're more than worth it." I nodded and watched him go in the bathroom. Everything about Shak is dangerous and off limits but I had to have him.

"Let me get dressed." I yelled out to my sister. I stepped in the bathroom with him and he opened the glass door.

"You stay tempting me." He pulled me close and kissed me. This isn't the first time we've showered together. Hell, we sleep naked too. I'm so comfortable around him for some reason. If you're wondering; he is absolutely well endowed.

I'm not speaking 13 inches or anything like that but he's big, thick and long.

"If you can keep your hands off me, I know you can do it with any naked woman." He threw his head back laughing.

"No other woman has made me keep my hands off."

"Whatever." I grabbed the soap and he held my waist.

"I'm not saying it to upset you. I've never lied to you and I'm not about to, just to appease you."

"You're right." I handed him the soap when I finished, washed up and left him in there. I can't even get mad because he's always been real with me. Maybe because I'm feeling him a lot. Not in a love type of way. It's too early but more like I wanna be territorial.

"So you mad?"

"No. I'm good." I slid my leg in my jeans and did the same with the other. I grabbed my shirt and put it on as well. I didn't care to put lotion on or anything. I wanted to get away from him so the faster I get dressed, the better. I turned and he was sitting on the bed in a towel staring at me.

"I'm gonna stop coming over."

"What?"

"You obviously have strong feelings for me whether you tell me or not and I'm not about to let you pressure me into doing anything."

"Shak." He stood and shushed me with his fingers.

"You know I want you but I also understand why you're holding back. I'm not mad and when I'm ready, if you're still available I'll take you away." He moved and grabbed his things.

"I don't wanna not see you."

"But seeing me and knowing what I'm doing isn't fair to you either." He put his clothes on. I sat on the bed waiting for him to say, *sike, he's playing* or something but those words never came as he collected all his stuff; including his tooth brush.

"I'll see you around." He kissed my forehead and walked out my room and life. I wanted to scream for him to come back but I deserve better. If I find it without him then we were never meant to be.

"You ready?" C'Yani walked out the kitchen.

"What's wrong?"

"Is it obvious?"

"Well yes. Your eyes are watery and you're watching Shak leave. Did something happen?"

"We can talk over food." She left it alone and we left to eat.

****

"You think I'm stupid for making him do all those things first?" C'Yani and I were out shopping in Short Hills mall. They put in a brand-new Louboutin store and I wanted to see if they had the same shoes online in the store.

"Look at these and no." She lifted a pair of all red shoes. They reminded me of Christmas because of how bright they were.

"He's probably used to getting his way and he can't with you. Sis, I know you really like him but if it's meant to be, it will."

"What about with you and Meek?" Someone cleared their throat before she could answer and we turned around. It was three women and one is very familiar.

"You need to leave Shak alone." The closer she got, I realized she's the chick from the club.

"Barb is that you?"

"Barb?" My sister started laughing.

"Yea bitch it's me."

"Bitch?"

"That's what I said. I'm giving you a warning to leave him alone."

"Who says I'm with him?"

"I followed him to your house." One chick said proudly.

"Ok stalker." She gave me a fake smile.

"No need to worry ladies. He told me earlier he's not ready to settle down, therefore; you have nothing to worry about."

"We ain't worried. You should be."

"Why is that?" C'Yani stood on the side of me. She can't fight but she won't let them jump me either.

"Because two of us are pregnant." My heart sank listening to her.

142

"You'll never be first in his life sweetie because we are."

"Ok then. Do me a favor and let him know you told me. That way he'll be made aware never to contact me again. Look, I'm blocking him as we speak." I showed them my phone, not like I had to but I wanted each one to know I'm done. I knew about the chicks but if he's sleeping with them raw and putting babies in them, maybe it's best we stay apart.

"You ok Teri?" C'Yani asked when we got to the car. After they left the store, I grabbed her hand and we went in the opposite direction. I didn't want them to know what they said bothered me.

"Yup. We going out tonight." I'm gonna show him I can do the same. Well not pop out babies but be around other niggas.

I walked in the ho house and music was blasting. I call it that because it's where I kept the main bitches I slept with. It's no secret I'm a ho and proud of it. I can't find it in me to settle down with tons of pussy floating around. I mean bitches just giving it away and looking for men to take it. The only person who's ever made me think about settling is Teri. I don't know what it is about her but when we're around one another, shit is peaceful.

I didn't wanna leave her the way I did but she left me no choice. I'm aware that she doesn't wanna share me but being with different women is how we met. Maybe I should've never pursued her but who the hell knew she'd want more? I know eventually I'm gonna have to step up or she'll seek out another and I'm not having it.

Teri is beautiful, smart, has her own everything and all she wants is me. However; it's not something I'm willing to give her and I respect her enough not to try and sleep with her. I'm not saying I don't want to but she's requesting STD tests and shit. I'ma safe ass nigga when it comes to sex.

I walked up the steps in search of the girls, opened the door with the music playing and watched Barb devour the hell outta Cheryl, who's got Tasha sitting on her face. I stripped out my clothes, put two condoms on and bulldozed my way inside Barb. I could tell she appreciated the effort because she threw her ass back.

"Fuck Shak. You feel so good." She moaned out and I felt her creaming on my dick.

"Come here Tasha." She hopped off Cheryl, came over and dropped to her knees. She could suck the shit outta my dick. Cheryl knew how to ride me until I came and Barb overall, had the best out the three. How can I give this up?

"Fuck me Shak. Yes. Yes. Yessssss." Cheryl moaned out as I hit it from the back, while Barb sucked on my balls. I'm telling you we stayed in the room for three hours fucking the shit outta one another. It's never been a time we didn't leave fully satisfied.

I went in the bathroom, flushed the condom down the toilet and walked in the stand-up shower. Tonight, I'm supposed to meet these guys who wanna work with me. One runs an urgent care and the other guy is from up north. Both of them wanted to dabble in the pill distribution business. I'm not selling dope or any shit like that. It's too easy to get caught. The pill business is where the money's at.

"Can I talk to you?" Cheryl came in and passed me the wife beater on my bed.

"What up?"

"Two things." I continued getting dressed as she stood there.

"Waiting."

"I found someone and I'm moving out." I shrugged my shoulders and told her good luck. None of these women were hostages and could leave at any time.

"It's one of the guys who work for you and I know you don't care but can we keep this arrangement between us?" I walked over to her.

"You really like him?" She smiled and nodded.

"My lips are sealed. Make sure he treats you good." Cheryl is probably the nicest outta the other two. She doesn't get in any arguments with them and on nights she hears me fucking one of the other women because it's not always threesomes, she never got upset. Barb and Tasha on the other hand went at it every time. They wouldn't do it when I was here but Cheryl would send me a video. *Crazy right?*

"As of right now he is."

"Good. What's the second thing?" I sat down and put my new Jordan's on. She was struggling to get it out.

"WHAT?" She jumped.

"We were at the mall the other day and Barb told some woman you impregnated her and Tasha."

"Why the fuck she say that?" I grabbed my shirt and tossed it across my shoulder.

"I have no clue. You could tell the woman was hurt even though she tried to hide it." I opened the door and ran my hand over my head praying the answer to my next question isn't what I think.

"What did the woman look like?" She smirked.

"She was gorgeous and so was the woman with her. She had hazel eyes and a shirt that read sexy." I instantly got mad and stormed out the room. It had to be Teri and I'm sure Barb recognized her from the club.

"Shak please don't say anything. At least not until I'm gone." She stood in front of me with her hand on my chest.

"You like the woman."

"It doesn't matter now because I'm sure she hates me after hearing that shit."

"Look. I'm going to the club and if she's there I'll let her know they lied. But Shak you have to give this up." She pointed to the house.

"No woman will ever be ok allowing her man to sleep with others or have a house like this."

"I like this shit though." I laughed.

"Yea well the woman won't and if you try to hide it with Barb and Tasha around, she's bound to find out." I went in the room to grab my wallet and keys.

"You need help moving?"

"I don't have a lot and..."

"Send me the address and I'll furnish the place for you."

"No Shak. I have enough money saved up from working. My furniture will be delivered in two days."

"A'ight. Call me if you need anything."

"I will and don't mess with her heart. If you're not ready, leave her alone."

"Bye." I kissed her cheek and left. Barb tried speaking to me but if I responded I'd probably wring her fucking neck for lying.

I pulled up to the club at the same time my cousin Meek did. The two of us stepped in through the back and it was packed, which meant money is being made. I wasn't sure about opening one of these because it's a ton of clubs out here. I'm happy I did though. I made great money here and the few other spots I owned.

When your father dies and leaves the kind of money mine did, it's best to invest. That way it's harder for the feds to claim you're into illegal shit.

We made our way through the crowd and bitches were everywhere. Some barely had clothes on. Meek and I looked at each other and grinned. We knew the chicks wouldn't have any problems going home with us. New pussy is fun that's for sure.

"Boss, the guys are waiting upstairs." I don't usually conduct business here but they wanted to see the place. I went to them and some chick stood in front of the one guy.

"What's your number?" The guy pulled his phone out and once she turned around I yanked her up.

"She ain't got no phone. Tha fuck you doing Teri?"

"Get off me." I noticed hurt in her eyes.

"Let me talk to you real quick. Meek, I'll be right back." He nodded and I grabbed her arm tight and didn't let go until we were in the bathroom. I locked the door and stared at her.

"Why you in that nigga face?"

"You don't have the right to ask me anything."

"And why is that?"

"One... you left the house saying we needed to stay away from each other. Two... your ho approached me about having your kid with her and the other woman."

150

"Teri, I don't sleep with them without condoms." She walked closer to me and pressed her lips on mine.

"And three... even though it may not be true, nothing is hurting me more than seeing two hickeys on your neck." I didn't bother covering them up.

"You needed pussy bad huh?" She shook her head in disgust.

"Teri."

"All you did is prove you're not ready to settle down and you'll always have women to sleep with." Her eyes were watery.

"Goodbye Shak." She pushed me out the way and left me standing alone. I knew the hickeys were there and forgot about them. I had no idea she'd be here otherwise I would've covered them up. I left the bathroom and found the two guys talking to Meek. I joined the conversation, gave them the information and made plans to contact them with the shipping dates.

"Get the hell off me." I heard and turned to see some guy all over Teri. You could tell she was uncomfortable. I mean he had his hands on her ass and squeezing it. I walked

over and tapped the guy on his shoulder.

"Bro, she doesn't want you touching her."

"Mind yo business nigga." Dude barked without

turning around.

"Teri you want him touching you?" She shook her head

no.

"You heard her. Back the fuck up."

"Fuck you punk." I knocked him out and continued

stomping his ass out.

"Shak I'm ok. That's enough." I heard her but my anger

got the best of me. Before I knew it, his friends came over and

it was a brawl. I can't even tell you who did what because once

the gun went off it was mayhem. So much for having a good

night.

"Who we fucking up now?" My cousin Fazza said when Shakim and I stepped in the house. We took a ride out to Delaware to find out if they heard who the dudes were, we stomped out. They had way more connects than we did.

"I can't even tell you who those niggas were." I said.

"What were y'all fighting for?" I glanced over at Shak.

"He was all in some chick face and she wasn't beat."

"Oh my God. Say it ain't so." Fazza's wife came in the room grinning.

"What?"

"ZIAAAAAA!" She shouted to Mazza's wife who walked in with a bag of food.

"Why you screaming? Hey boys."

"Boys? We men and you better not be letting my cousins touch you." Shakim always said Ty is his wife and Zia is the side chick. He's been saying it since we were kids. I may have lived 3000 miles away but my summers and holidays have been in Jersey.

"Whatever. I miss y'all." She kissed both of our cheeks and sat down.

"I think Shakim done found a woman." Zia snapped her neck.

"I ain't find nobody."

"Shakim, I know you and there's no way in hell you're approaching a dude for a woman you don't like. You have security for that."

"Awww cuz. I know she ain't pussy whipped you already."

"Fazza don't act like you weren't whipped after the first lick." Ty and him always argued.

"I wasn't. Now if you say after you first juggled my balls in your mouth, I'd agree."

"Let me juggle them right now. I bet my teeth will crush 'em like candy."

"I bet you don't suck this big dick no more."

"Yea right." She waved him off.

"Is she pretty? Wait! I hope she's not one outta that ho house you and Meek keep them at."

154

"Yo Zia, why I gotta be put in the middle? This his shit." I dug in her tray and took one of the chicken wings out. I did fuck the chicks over there but not the main ones. It's usually when he has BBQ's or we take them home from the club.

"What I tell you about eating off my wife nigga?" Mazza punched me in the chest.

"She loves me." Zia leaned over and kissed my cheek again.

"Zia don't get fucked up."

"Anyway. Babe, Shakim found a chick."

"Stop saying that." He moved out the chair and walked outside.

"Is he really that mad?"

"Yup! The chick doesn't want anything to do with him because she ain't down with him having the house. Then, Barb told her he's expecting kids from her and Tasha and last but not least. He left the woman's house, told her he'd give her space and popped up at the club with two hickeys. She won't take his calls or open the door to see him."

"Why he ain't kick the door in?"

"Mazza, everything doesn't have to include bullying."

"It's not bullying. He wants to talk and she doesn't. He's just making her listen." All of us looked at him and busted out laughing.

"Anyway, you have to bring her by so we can meet her." Zia waved him off and continued eating.

"Now, how am I gonna do that when she ain't even talking to him?" Fazza and Mazza both did a gesture with their heads for me to follow them outside. Shakim was smoking with his head back on the lawn chair.

"Dude you fought or should I say put in the hospital, is from Connecticut. He's supposedly high on the food chain and came to Jersey for a wedding." Shak shrugged his shoulders.

"The groom is the guy you beat up." Mazza pointed to me and handed us an envelope. Fazza snatched the blunt outta Shak's hand and asked how he smoking in his house and not sharing? Always comedy when they around each other.

"Long story short, keep your eyes and ears to the streets. They're no longer around but you know they'll be back. If that's the case, you already know how we get down." Mazza finished talking and went in the house because Zia called him.

"We can roll up there and get it popping. Let me know." Fazza spoke and left the two of us outside.

"What you wanna do?" He asked me and I shrugged.

"I'm down with whatever."

"A'ight lets go back to Jersey and get the team onboard." I nodded and we took the short drive from Delaware back home. I dropped him off, went to my place, showered and headed out. There's one place I needed to be and it had to be tonight.

DING DONG. I still can't believe they had this shitty doorbell. It sounds like Christmas songs are playing when you press it.

"Hey. She's upstairs." I looked at Teri and she seemed to be as sad as Shak.

"You good?"

"Yup. Perfect." She gave me a fake smile.

"Ugh, should I leave?" She smirked.

"Nah but you should definitely turn music on." I glanced around their place.

"I'll only fuck her all over my house. Y'all got too much going on over here." She mushed me and locked the door.

"Her room is the last one on the left." I told her thanks and walked up the stairs. C'Yani had no idea I was coming and I'm happy because the booty shorts and tank top she has on is easier to remove. If she knew I was here, she'd probably put more clothes on. I swear she's corny.

I closed the door and walked behind her as she picked clothes out. I kissed the back of her neck.

"What are you doing here?" She snatched the robe off her bed to cover up. I took it and tossed it on the floor.

"I hoped you would come to me but it's fine. I'm about to turn you the fuck out." I pulled her close, lifted the tank top up, and slid the shorts down her leg. C, had a banging body. I could stare at her all day.

"You want me C?" I kicked my sneakers off and removed my shirt.

"I do but..." My tongue slid across her lips.

"But what?"

"I'm not as experienced."

"Don't worry ma. I'm fluent in the sheets." She welcomed my tongue a few seconds later and we engaged in a kiss that woke my man right up.

"I've wanted you ever since the day at the hospital." She silently said as I laid her on the bed and began making love to her breasts. They were plump and juicy, just the way I liked. As I kissed down the rest of her body, she shivered.

"Can you go down on me again?" I chuckled a little and stood.

"Not until you say, I want my pussy ate. Or can you eat my pussy." She covered her mouth.

"It sounds so.-"

"It sounds sexy as fuck. Say it." She shook her head no a few times.

I let two of my fingers roam up and down her pussy and refused to put my mouth on her until she said it. I could feel her clit swelling as I circled it.

"Meek, please."

"Say it C."

"I can't. It's not me." I circled faster and her body began grinding on my hand.

"Say it." I guess she had enough of me teasing her.

"GOT DAMMIT. I WANT YOU TO EAT MY FUCKING PUSSY MEEK. EAT IT UNTIL I CUM IN YOUR MOUTH. SHIT, I NEED IT." She screamed out. Her hands were above her head, body slightly arched and I could see her treasure pulsating. I spread her legs, held on to her thighs and gave her exactly what she begged for.

"Cum for me C." Her hands were pulling on my dreads as she fucked my face. I don't even think she realized how much I was enjoying it myself.

"Yesssss. Oh shittt. Yessssss." Her cream oozed out and in my mouth. Instead of giving her a minute, I continued and had her pleading for a nigga to stop. I finished after the fourth one, kissed up her body and stuck my tongue in her mouth. My dick rubbed against her pussy and she wrapped her legs around my waist.

"I want you to teach me how to please you." I stopped sucking on her neck and stared.

"We may not be a couple but if I teach you, you better not show any other man; including your ex."

"Never." She smiled and pulled me in for another kiss.

"Fuck me Meek."

"I'm about to and don't stop me."

"I won't. Fuckkkkkkkk!" She screamed out once I pushed my way through her tunnel. If I didn't know any better, I'd say she was a damn virgin. She was extra tight and wet. I noticed her eyes closed and had her reopen them.

"Watch this nigga take you to ecstasy." She nodded and kept them open as much as she could. I spread her legs open and had her sit up.

"Take your fingers and play with your clit while I'm fucking you."

"In front of you?" She questioned.

"Yup. Do it." She started and bit down on her lip as the pressure began building.

"Mmm hmm. You doing good ma. Now keep going so you can feel the difference cumming all over my dick." She nodded, circled faster and not too long after screamed out again. I gotta teach her not to yell as loud. I don't mind but her sister doesn't need to hear.

"Let me see you on top." And just like that she said, she was finished.

"Nah. You're never gonna learn if you stop." I sat on the edge of the bed, took both of her hands and out them on my shoulder, spread her legs and had her body go down slow.

"It's my first time." She may as well be a virgin because she was clueless as fuck.

"Don't worry." Pain etched on her face.

"If you think it's gonna hurt, it will and there won't be any enjoyment."

"Ok. Ok. I'll try." She didn't move.

"Kiss me." I slowly rocked her hips back and forth and in circles. Even though I'm helping her, it felt real good.

"Stand and drop." She nodded and did it but not fast.

"Oh my gawdddd, it feels good." Her head went back as she began getting into it. I scooted further back on the bed and had her get on her knees.

"Try it on your own." I placed my hands behind my head and watched her pussy inhale my dick.

"Damn C. Mmph." I bit down on my lip and tried my hardest not to cum. I don't know who taught her how to squeeze those muscles but I was losing the fight to hold my nut. Both of us were moaning for the other and it just happened.

"Oh shit C." I released inside by accident.

"What?"

"I came in you. I'm sorry."

"I'm on the pill but we need to use protection next time."

"You right." I lifted up on my elbows and she still had my soft dick in her.

"How did I do?"

"Your pussy is good regardless of you just learning. Don't worry though; we got all night."

"All night? You can do it again?" I laughed.

163

"Yes and so can you."

"I don't know." I flipped her over and went down on her again. She and I definitely had a long night.

"What you doing? Sssss." Meek asked as I let my hands go up and down his shaft. I tried giving head to Ty but it didn't feel right. He wasn't coaching me and I felt weird doing it.

"I wanna learn how to do this." I opened my mouth and slowly licked the tip. I pulled out and it sounded like a lollipop.

"Keep going." I felt him watching me and tried being sexy. My ass started gagging and I felt a little vomit coming up.

"Don't pretend to be a pro. It takes time to learn the craft C." I nodded and tried again. This time I spit on it like he told me, to make it wetter.

"Go faster and stroke me at the same time." I did it and once his hand fell on the back of my head, I knew he was satisfied.

"Keep going ma. Shitttttttt." His leg began to shake and his dick did something weird in my mouth.

"I'm about to cum C and you ain't ready for that."

"Let me see." I went faster and sucked harder.

165

"GOT DAMNNN!!!!" He shouted and a milky substance went in my mouth. It wasn't a bad taste so I continued sucking until he was completely soft. He yanked me up by my hair and I yelled out. No man has ever manhandled me so I was nervous.

"Now that was some banging ass head." He slipped his tongue in my mouth and had me lay on top of him. He taught me how to please him a week ago and the two of us have been sexing everyday. My coochie is extra sore but once he goes down the pain goes away. Today is the first time I went to please him and I enjoyed it.

"I'm glad you liked it." I felt him hardening under me.

"You ok to ride?" He asked and never waited for my answer as he lifted my body and mounted me on top.

"Doesn't matter now. Oh shoooot Meek." I was leaning back, with my hands gripping his legs, going up and down.

"You a pro now ma. Fuck me." I smiled and went up, dropped down and did the things he taught me on top.

"C. You feel good." I enjoyed hearing him moan out my name.

"Make me cum baby." His fingers rubbed over my pearl slow, then fast and the pressure intensified.

"I'ma cum with you." He sat up, pulled me close and began sucking on my breasts.

"I'm cumming Meek."

"Keep going ma." I went faster and felt him thrusting harder under me.

"Meeekkkkkkk!" I dug my nails in his shoulder as the massive current overtook me. I rested my head on his shoulder and closed my eyes.

"I hope that pill works well because the amount of cum I let off in you, should make you pregnant each time." I started laughing and silently prayed the pill was strong enough too. Both of us are careless as hell but the way he does my body makes him worth it.

****

"Come on C. Let's go get the test done." He patted my ass and raised me off his soft dick. It felt funny sliding out and I'll never get over seeing how white it gets from me.

"Can we go tomorrow? I'm tired."

"You said that yesterday." He carried me in the bathroom and started the shower for us.

"I can look at your body all day C." I felt shy under his eyes for some reason.

"You're beautiful and it's too bad he didn't take the time out to really know you." He pecked my lips and started washing up.

"What do you mean?"

"He may know where you work, how much money you make and even how to fuck him a little but he doesn't know the real you."

"The real me?"

"The woman behind the uppity look. The woman who did any and everything to please a man who wasn't worthy. A woman who was scared to explore her own body until I stepped in. And a woman who managed to take her nose out the air to politic with real people." I didn't know what to say.

"C'Yani your heart is very pure and I can see the innocence in you as well. However; you put that pride aside to learn how to please me and I know it was hard. You told me

168

things I should've been privy too only if we knew each other longer." He was right.

After the first night we had sexual intercourse he and I spoke about so many things. I learned he has a construction company and helps his cousin when needed. He broke up with his ex, almost a year ago and he says she's crazy. I would be too if he sexed me like that all the time.

"You're a good and bougie woman who let this thug nigga turn her out."

"I definitely did." I wrapped my arms around his neck.

"Whatever you need, I got you C and that's real shit." I planted my lips on his. I loved kissing him.

"I got you too baby. Oh wait! Is it ok to call you that?"

"Call me whatever you want as long as it ain't another nigga." He and I finished washing up, got dressed and went down to my doctor's office. The first time we had sex, I woke up the next day and requested an STD test. He overheard me and made me add him too. I was a little offended because I didn't have anything and I've only been with one man but then

again, I understood. We didn't know each other and were
reckless.

****

"Ok. The results don't come back for two weeks but the
rapid HIV test returned negative for both of you. As long as the
other ones are negative too, I don't see it being a problem
having unprotected sex if it's only you two."

"It's only me, right?" I asked sitting on his lap. The
nurse stepped out the room to give us privacy.

"Yup. Come on. I'm hungry." We walked out and
headed to our cars. We drove separate because he was going
somewhere but I guess he changed his mind.

"Ummm. Should I be worried?" Someone spray painted
I love you and *I'll never leave you alone* on his truck.

"Nah. It's my ex and she know not to come around. We
can take your car."

"You're just gonna leave your truck?"

"I'll have the tow people come pick it up."

"Ok then. Where we going?"

"Don't matter to me." I pulled off and noticed a woman standing down the street. She kept looking in the parking lot we came out of. It had to be the ex. I thought about telling Meek but I don't want him killing anyone while I'm around. If she showed up here, I'm sure she'll catch him elsewhere.

I parked at a restaurant on the beach and went to pay the meter. Meek stopped me and took it upon himself to put in enough for six hours. I asked why and he told me after we ate, he wanted to walk in some of the stores. I damn near had to pull Tyrone's teeth to get him shopping with me and Meek had no problem. He took my hand in his and opened the door for me.

"What up Meek?" Some young white guy spoke and slapped hands with him.

"Not much. Let me get a table by the window."

"Sure. Follow me."

"You know him?"

"I have a repore with people you'd never imagine."

"Really?" He pulled the chair out for me.

171

"I know how to be professional too C." He sat across from me.

"I wasn't insinuating anything."

"The funny part is I know you weren't. I've known you for a short time and can tell when you're being smart or totally clueless." I gasped and hit him with my menu.

"I do. What you eating?" I glanced over the menu and ordered shrimp with steak and French fries. I loved them. He ordered a hefty steak and other stuff to go along with it. He stared at me and I became extremely uncomfortable.

"What?"

"You tryna be my woman or what?"

"Is that how you ask?" I folded my arms.

"I could ask while you're riding my dick but then I'd miss you acting like a baby." I poked my lips out and he leaned over to kiss them. I grabbed his face and sucked on the bottom one.

"I'll be your woman if you let me use whip cream on you with strawberries." I thought he'd fall out the chair from laughing.

"As long as you're not sticking anything in my ass baby, nothing is off limits when it comes to you."

"It's not?"

"No and where did that even come from?" The waitress sat his salad in front of him. She also placed stuff mushrooms and crab nachos on the table as appetizers.

"I was looking on ways to be sexy in the bedroom." He laughed.

"Try this." He lifted a nacho and fed it to me.

"Mmmmm. That's real good babe." He used his thumb to wipe the sauce off my lip.

"I can't believe you enjoy seafood and never had them." It was true. I enjoyed seafood but only ate shrimp and lobster. I was too scared to venture out and try other things. Looks as if he's about to have me trying a lot of stuff.

"Oooh, that's hot." I bit down on the mushroom and burnt my tongue.

"Why you think I didn't ask you to try it yet?"

"You're mean."

"I'll never be mean to you again." I blushed.

"I'll try and be hood for you."

"No thanks."

"Why not? If you're making sacrifices why can't I?" I placed another nacho in my mouth.

"I like you're high sadity attitude."

"Whatever." I moved back as the waitress placed our food in front of us.

"To new beginnings ma." He lifted the drink the waitress brought. I did the same and we kissed as the glasses clinked together.

"I thought you weren't with him." Ty said. Meek continued cutting his steak. I guess giving me the floor to answer.

"Ty, my business is none of your concern."

"He's not your type. Why are you lowering your standards?" Meek's face got tight.

"Say what you wanna say and bounce motherfucker. If you disrespect her or talk that dumb shit about me, I'm gonna lay yo ass out." He put another piece of steak in his mouth.

"What do you want Ty?"

"We'll speak another time."

"No you won't." Meek stood and towered over Ty.

"I get this is the first time you've seen her in a while and needed to ask questions but let it be the last time you part your lips to even say hello."

"You can't tell me who I can speak to." Meek chuckled and not even two seconds later, Ty was on the ground. What's mind boggling is how no one said a word. No cameras, no one threatening to contact the police or anything.

"Get this motherfucker outta here. He's disturbing me and my woman." Two men rushed over to pick Ty up. I had no words.

"For future reference, don't ever entertain a man who not only did you wrong but questioned your choice." I could tell she was at a loss for words.

"Eat your food ma. It's a store I wanna go in." I picked my fork up and continued eating.

"Try this now that it cooled off." She opened her mouth and ate the stuffed mushroom. I think she was scared but she had nothing to worry about.

"You like it?" She nodded.

"Ma, this is new to you so I understand why you're afraid but have no worries. I won't put my hands on you. Now enjoy your meal." She lifted the fork and started to eat. It took her some time but she finally spoke again.

"This scene is beautiful." She stared out the window drinking the wine.

"It's my favorite spot."

"You come here a lot?"

"Enough to have the table available upon my arrival."

"Wow. Who are you?"

"I feel we're a little past introductions, but my name is Mekhi Gibson and the streets call me Meek. I'm 26, born and raised in California until the untimely death of my mother."

"I know all that silly." She smiled.

"I'm talking about the fact you have a reserved table when you're not here. No one moved when you knocked my ex out and everyone seems to love you wherever we go."

"My construction business has led me to meeting some infamous people. I've done jobs for politicians, the mob, crooked niggas, cops and the list goes on. In order to get respect, you have to give it and I demand that shit. My cousin and I also have various investments that require me to interact with others. I'm not as ghetto and dumb as outsiders assume."

"I never said that."

"Not you ma. But on a daily basis I'm stereotyped by my clothes and appearance. Unless I'm speaking proper, I must be a hood nigga." She gave me a sad look.

"It used to bother me but not anymore. I'll never get over the faces I see when people find out I'm the head nigga in charge. They're so used to the white man taking over everything, they don't know how to react."

"I feel like we're one in the same besides our gender and I don't own anything."

"We are and you can own whatever you want."

"I wouldn't even know what to own." I had her sit on my lap and stared in her eyes.

"You can start with your own advertising firm. It will be slow in the beginning but I know people in high places who either owes me a favor or looking for new ideas to expand their business."

"You'd help me?"

"Hell yea I would. You're my woman and depending on how long we're together we can take both of our businesses to an entirely different level." She turned around and straddled me in front of everyone.

"You tryna fuck in here because that skirt is rising and so is my man." She had a sneaky grin on her face.

"If it were dark, I'd do it." Her hand slid in my sweats and massaged me.

"Get up." I smacked her ass and we stood.

"Let's go."

"Wait! We didn't pay."

"And we won't. This my shit." Her mouth fell open as I held the door. I could tell she had questions but never asked. I appreciated it because I hated for people to inquire about my life. Let me be the one to bring it up.

****

"Get something nice." I told her in the lingerie store. I came in here once for Kim but never purchased anything. I wanted to but she'd find a way to piss me off and I'd change my mind.

"The prices are outrageous for these small pieces."

"Seeing you in them will be worth it." She walked over to me.

"Now that I've learned how to please you, I'm gonna go harder every time. I want you to be strung out off me, like I am with you." I had her stand in front of me.

"You strung out C?"

"You have no idea babe."

"Tell me."

"The moment you made me cum at the cemetery I've envisioned us as one. I mean, I wanted you at the hospital and even played with myself afterwards, but to actually feel the pleasure you brought out, had me hooked. In your office is when I knew you'd be the man who'd do my body right and after having you, I don't want anyone else to touch, kiss or make love to me. You are the only man I desire and that's some real shit." I had a grin on my face. I almost laughed when she said *real shit* but I knew it was her way of expressing how she truly felt in her own hood way.

"We on the same page sexy."

"You sure because I'm not as experienced. -" I shushed her with my lips.

"Never compare yourself to another woman. If you haven't noticed, every person is different and will show you other things and you've done that."

"You too. Let me see what else I want." She pecked my lips and finished browsing the store. By the time we stopped shopping it was after nine and a few thousand dollars later. I didn't mind because the majority of it is for my eyes only.

✶✶✶✶✶✶✶✶✶✶✶✶✶✶✶✶✶✶✶✶✶✶

"I'm going to look at a few buildings tomorrow. Do you want to come?" C asked on the phone. I was outta town but she and I spoke everyday.

"I won't be home until Monday but you can FaceTime me."

"Meek, I don't want to go alone."

"You're not. Teri's going and I'll have someone watching you."

"Meek?"

"I told you my ex is crazy and I refuse to let her catch you slipping. Plus, you can't fight baby so I have to." She sucked her teeth but it's the truth. I asked if she wanted to learn and couldn't stop laughing at the stance she'd get in. She gave up and won't let me show her anymore.

"FINE! But if it's nice should I take it?"

"C'Yani, look at all of them and don't give the realtor a yes until you're sure."

"How will I know?"

"When I got my building for the construction company I went to see tons of places. None of them were good enough but when the right one came along I felt it in my gut. If you get that feeling then it's the spot for you."

"Got it. Gut feeling, buy it."

"Bye C. I'll call you later." I hung up laughing while Shak had a tight face.

"I told you to come with me when I go over there."

"I ain't tryna force her to talk to me." I gave him the side eye.

"Fuck it. I'll go when we return. Is that him?" He pointed to the guy he beat up. We took a ride to Connecticut with lil Faz and Mystic to stake out the place. Shak had a team but we're family, and knew if anything went down no one would think twice about reacting.

For two days we've been here and he's been to his mother's house, a few chicks and I'm guessing a trap house. Nothing about him screamed BOSS but you didn't know that about us either. We lived nice and all but we aren't the flaunting type, where some dudes are. If the guy decided to come for revenge we know he'd run back and if we monitored him for a few days we'd know exactly where he'd go.

"Yup."

"A'ight. Let's stay one more night and head back."

"Thought we were staying longer." Mystic asked.

"We were until Meek told him to stop by and see his precious Teri." Lil Faz always had jokes. He's definitely his father's child. His twin sister can't stand the way he acts and gets into all the time with him. Mystic is the younger brother who came not even a year later.

"Fuck y'all." He caught an attitude. I pulled off and drove to get something to eat. I was hungry as hell.

"Why she calling?" The call was from Jasmine. I hadn't spoken to her since the last time we fucked, which was two years ago. I answered to see what she wanted.

"Hey boo. Can I see you?"

"Not at all bitch. Don't hit this line again." I disconnected the call and continued about my business. I wasn't cheating on C for no bitch.

"Yo, there goes the guy again." Mystic pointed to them staring at us in the soul food spot. None of us reacted and kept calm to make them think we didn't know they were watching us.

"We're gonna go out here, get in the car and leave. Any shit pop off, y'all already know what it is." Shak spoke and each of us made sure our weapons were loaded.

"Here you go." I paid the girl at the counter, each of us grabbed our food and walked out.

BEEP! BEEP! I hit the alarm on the truck and all of us got in.

"These niggas are straight punks." Shak and I both smiled and nodded our heads at them. It's our way of letting the enemy know we knew exactly whip they were.

"If they ain't busting off, I'm about to eat." I kept my eye in the rearview mirror and noticed the guy stull standing there. He didn't make a move or nothing. What type of gangsta's are they? We made it back to the hotel, ate our food, changed clothes and drove back home. We did what we needed to and I'm sure we'll be back.

184

"What's wrong?" Teri asked when I slammed my phone on the table. We were at the diner waiting on her stuck-up sister who claims to have great news.

"Nothing. I'm good." Ever since I saw her out to eat with Meek, I've been in my feelings. Not because she is obviously messing with him but because I noticed how attentive he was to her. Feeding her off his fork, he sat her on his lap and even knocked Ty out.

Yea, I was at the place with him but that's not the point. No one knew we were there and it pissed me off to see Ty get upset. Like how you mad when you're here with me? I guess he didn't think she'd move on but after the way she lost her child and him not being there, I had no doubt she would never be with him again. However; she's with the man I've wanted for two years.

Meek isn't like most niggas and as ruthless as he may be, he has a good heart. He never allowed men to disrespect me when I stripped or passed out bottles and his stroke game is ridiculous. I know for a fact her ugly ass can't handle him.

From what Ty says, not only is she boring but never tried new things. I know for a fact Meek loves a woman on top and can suck him off good. He's not the type to train a bitch either; or is he?

C'Yani stepped in looking like a brand-new woman. I haven't seen her since she broke her ankle but I must say, she had a glow to her. Her skin wasn't pale anymore, she looks healthier than before and she was smiling. Whatever Meek did must have her in good spirits.

I am pissed because I called him the other day and he hung up. I've been calling the past two days and he refuses to answer. It's been two years since we graced each other's' presence sexually but he's always taking me up on my offer.

"What's up sis?"

"Can I start you off with a drink?" The waitress asked her.

"Yes, I'll have a soda."

"What you pregnant?" I asked with a hint of sarcasm.

"No kids for me but thanks for being concerned." She gave me a fake smile and I was a little happy. That meant Meek is using protection if they are sleeping together.

"Anyway, I can't drink beer or liquor with my food if you must know. And I don't think I'll drink ever again after the last time."

"Yea, you acted like a fool with liquor in your system. We wouldn't want that happening again." I gave her a fake smile.

"No we wouldn't. I missed a lot of time at work but being in high positions you can work from home. Where do you work again?" She ordered her drink and food and looked at Teri. I wanted to smack the fuck outta her but I didn't want to beat her ass in front of her sister.

"Anyway, my new man told me to look into buildings so I can start my own business." I rolled my eyes listening to her mention Meek. I don't know why she didn't say his name.

"Ok. Keep going." Teri rolled her hand in a circle.

"Since you backed out at the last minute helping me, I went on my own."

"I'm sorry sis. I had a lot going on with my job and…"

"It's fine." You could tell by C'Yani's face, she was hurt but as usual she kept it to herself. One thing I can say about her is, she never comes outta character.

"So yesterday I found the perfect spot. Oh my God Teri, it's huge with four floors. I figured you could have a floor for your business, one floor will be for conferences and things like that and another one can be for a cafeteria and some food chains."

"Oh my God sis. I'm proud of you." The two embraced and I gave her a fake smile.

"I have the keys so we can go look whenever."

"Let's go after we eat." She glanced at me.

"I'll have to decline. Your friend doesn't appear interested so we can go tomorrow."

"You don't mind do you Jasmine?"

"Not at all. We may not be friends but I'm all about celebrating." I lifted my drink and sipped. This bitch always blows my high.

****

189

"Wow C'Yani. This is nice." We went floor to floor listening to her describe the visions she had. The spot is nice as hell and I was low key hating. I wonder if Meek got this for her?

"I know right. Mommy is coming over to help me find furniture and things like that. You can do whatever you want on your floor." The two of them hugged and my phone started going off.

Ty: *I want to fuck you.* I smirked staring down at the message. If this bitch only knew.

"Hey babe." I looked up and there was Meek, the Shak guy who owned the new club in town, along with two other guys.

Meek leaned down to kiss her and you could see the tension between Shak and Teri. It doesn't look as if he's tryna hear it tho because he snatched my friend up and walked out. The other guys were looking around while Meek appeared to be lost in love or some shit.

"I thought you weren't coming back for a day or two."

"Let me find out you don't wanna see me."

"Always baby. Let me show you around." She took his hand and gestured for the other guys to follow them, then it hit me on who they were. Those are the cousins from Delaware whose father is crazier than them. I only remember because one of them has different color eyes. It looks spooky as hell too.

"What the fuck you looking at?" All of them turned around. I guess no one paid attention to me when they arrived.

"Why is she here?" Meek asked and waited for C'Yani to answer.

"You know she's Teri's friend."

"Yea but she ain't yours."

"Meek don't be mean and Faz and Mystic let me finish showing you."

"I don't like that bitch C."

"Faz, for the short time I've know you, you don't like anyone." She pushed him gently on the arm.

"Nah something is sneaky about her." He walked over and stood in my face. She shook her head and ignored my presence like she has since we got here.

"You may be fooling her but I know you grimy as shit. You got one time to fuck with her or Teri and I'ma pour acid on your body and watch you melt away." He gave me the once over and backed away. How the hell did this man know who I was? He ain't even from Jersey.

I sucked my teeth and went to search for my friend. She was nowhere in sight so I walked down to the next floor. I heard yelling and couldn't help but listen. Evidently, Shak is feeling her and willing to do whatever if she gives him another chance. I had no idea they slept together or the relationship was deep.

"Ouch." I shouted when my body was slammed against the wall.

"You think this is a fucking game?" Meek had me pinned in a corner, while the Mystic guy with him stood watch.

"What are you talking about?"

"Bitch, you called my phone tryna fuck and now you're here with her. I'm not Ty so you won't catch me slipping but if

you breathe a word to her about the past, I'll fucking kill you."
The guy handed him something.

"And just so you know this ain't a joke I'm gonna leave
you with something."

"Ahhhhh." I screamed but he quickly covered my
mouth.

"I'm not the one you wanna play with." He pushed me
to the ground and I looked down at my leg that had blood
leaking out. He wiped the knife off on my shirt, handed it back
to the guy and stood in front of me.

"Tell that nigga he better not ever approach C'Yani
again and the same goes for you." He started to walk away.

"If either women asks what happened to your leg, tell
them a nail was sticking out and you ran in to it." The tears
raced down as I took my belt off and tied it around my leg. He
thinks he won the battle but I'm gonna win the war. He already
let me know C'Yani is his weakness and wants to keep this
secret private. Oh, I'm going to have fun with this.

"Why you avoiding me Teri?" Shak had me hemmed up in one of the rooms on the third floor.

"Shak, you have three women at your beckoned call, possibly two fake babies on the way and you fucked them after leaving my house."

"What did you expect? Teri you walked into this with your eyes wide open. Sex with those women and others have never been a secret. I get you have feelings for me and the hickeys upset you but I told you we were giving each other space."

"Ok then why not let me give out my phone number?"

"Oh, because you ain't fucking no one." I moved him from in front of me.

"How you telling me to keep my legs closed and you're out there opening ones belonging to different women?"

"Regardless of what you assume, no man better not get in between these thighs." He made his way to me from across the room.

"No man better not kiss you like this." He grabbed my face and slid his tongue in my mouth.

"No man better not have you in any positions such as this." In one swift motion, my legs were wrapped around his waist.

"Sssss. Shak." His fingers were circling my clit over my jeans. The friction from the material on my panties didn't make it better.

"Damn, I wish you were sitting on my face so I could taste the sweetness about to leave your body.

"Oh shit Shak. Shit." My body was begging for him to help me release. My breathing became erratic and I started to shake.

"I'm ready for you Teri." I wanted to ask questions but my mouth was on his shoulders biting down as he pulled a huge orgasm out.

"Let me taste." Before I could protest his hands were in my jeans.

"Ahhh." He slipped two fingers inside and a bitch began fucking them like it was his dick.

"Stop ma. My fingers ain't my dick." He moved his fingers, slid them in his mouth and then kissed me.

"I'm taking you home with me." All I could do is shake my head yes.

"Yoooo, that bitch bleeding on the ground." Shak's cousin came running in just as I buttoned my jeans.

"My sister?" I questioned and he gave me a *yea right* look. Why did I ask that when Meek is here?

"The ho you came with." I tried to walk and see but my legs were weak as hell.

"You think this is bad; just wait. Daddy gonna make it where you're laid up in bed with me all day." I sucked my teeth. Whether I wanted to admit it or not, I'm happy he found me and even happier he's about to bless me with some dick.

We stepped in the hallway and Jasmine was on the floor crying. You could tell through her jeans she was cut or something. I asked Shak and Faz to lift her up and they both gave me a crazy look. Am I missing something? He better not have fucked her and not tell me.

It took me telling him I wasn't coming over for the two of them to lift her. They stood her up and I let her hold on to my shoulder as we walked to the elevator.

"What did you run in to? Jasmine it looks deep."

"I didn't run into anything. Meek..." Mystic stepped on and she shut up.

"What were you saying about Meek?" I asked.

"Nothing. I thought he saw me."

"Nah Meek's with his woman." The two of them had a stare off until the elevator stopped.

"Who are you?" I asked a big buff dude standing outside the building with a car door opened.

"Boss called me to take someone to the hospital." Jasmine stared at me.

"We good. I can take her."

"Not tonight Teri. We have unfinished business."

"Are you going to leave me?" Jasmine asked and I felt bad. I told the guy to wait.

"Shak, I know you want me as much as I want you but she's my friend."

197

"Fuck her." He said it loud enough for her to hear.

"Why don't you like her?"

"I told you the first day we met she's gonna be a problem and I still feel the same. Let's go." He tried to take my hand.

"Shak, I'm not going to leave her. She doesn't know the man and she's scared. Look, send me your address and when I feel she's ok, I promise to come by."

"Teri I'm not tryna hear...."

"I promise to suck you off so good you're gonna be begging me to stop." I put his finger in my mouth and circled my tongue around, then let my hand go in his jeans and started kissing him.

"You like the way I taste right?" I pulled my hand out now that he was semi erect.

"Teri.-"

"I promise, I got you." His hand went behind my head as he placed another kiss on my lips.

"You better. I'll have Faz drive behind you so the car is there."

"Oh shit. I'm driving the Tesla." He shouted and ran to it.

"You better not fuck my girl shit up either."

"Your girl. Nigga she don't even know if you can please her. Don't worry Teri, if he can't, trust that his cousin can." Shak ran after him.

"Can we go?"

"I'm sorry." I ran over and hopped in the back with her. The guy closed the door and I sent a text to my sister telling her where I was.

****

"Ma'am you sure it was a dirty nail?" The doctor asked Jasmine when she took the jeans off.

"It could've been something else." She said groggily. They gave her medicine for pain the minute she stepped in.

"It's pretty deep and due to you getting here late, it appears infection began to set already."

"Ok." And just like that she was knocked out.

"You're her friend, right?"

"Yes."

"Ok I'm gonna be honest with you. It appears to be a knife cut and not a nail."

"What do you mean?"

"I've seen plenty of patients come in after running into a nail or even being cut but one but this is too deep. Are you sure she didn't do this to herself?"

"She's not suicidal."

"Let me show you why I asked." He lifted the bandage up and the cut was indeed deep.

"The way the skin is open with a straight line shows me it was a knife. If you notice here, some of the meat appears to cut as well. Now unless she ran into a nail more than once, this was deliberately done."

"She's not going through anything that I know of. I'll ask when she gets up." He nodded and had the nurse bring in the stuff to clean and stitch her up. He gave her fifteen stitches and pumped her with an antibiotic though the IV.

"Is everything ok?" My sister walked in with Meek who had a snarl on his face. What is it about Jasmine that none of them like?

200

"He thinks she did it to herself." I relayed what the doctor told me to them.

"Why would she do that?"

"No idea. Do you know why Meek?" C turned to stare at him.

"Nope." The minute he said it in a non chalant tone, I knew he had an idea of what happened.

"How would he know?" He now had a smirk on his face.

"Just asking sis." I shook my head at him.

"Where's the bathroom?"

"You just went before we left." Meek told her and pointed to one down the hall.

"You pregnant?"

"NO!" They both spoke at the same time.

"Well damn." She walked off leaving the two of us.

"If we're together long enough she'll be pregnant but right now we having fun."

"She likes you a lot Meek."

"I know."

"No, I mean a whole lot. She was the same with Ty."
He sucked his teeth.

"I'm not saying it to offend you. I'm saying it because I already can tell she's falling hard for you and I wanna make sure you're not going to leave or cheat on her."

"You're right, I can tell too. She's a good woman Teri and as of right now I don't plan on going anywhere. As far as cheating; not gonna happen. I turned her into my personal nympho and freak."

"Disgusting."

"You have no idea the disgusting things we do to each other." I started laughing.

"Well no babies right now. She wants to start her own business and we both know it's going to be hard."

"Exactly but I should be telling you no babies because once Shak gets you, he ain't pulling out." He hit me with the peace sign and said they'd see me later. C'Yani and Jasmine don't care for each other and he only brought her because she had to make sure everything was fine. Jasmine better appreciate it and stop acting like she hates my sister.

I looked down at my phone and it was the address from Shak. It's not the one where the ho house is. I wouldn't go anyway. Everyone knew of that spot because not only did those women stay there, he threw parties and BBQ's in the place.

I sent him a message saying I'd be there shortly and waited for Jasmine to wake up so I could take her home. My horny ass was excited to receive some dick so she better hurry up or I'm leaving.

I answered the door for Teri and smiled seeing her in a long coat. It doesn't take a rocket scientist to know she's either naked underneath or has something sexy on. Instead of waiting, I locked the door and removed the jacket to witness exactly what I thought. She had on tight black one piece. My man woke straight up as she turned to reveal the entire front was sheer.

We've seen one another naked a bunch of times but it's different now. We're about to cross the line and ain't no turning back. She knew I was turned on and reciprocated a smile herself. Now me wanting to make sure I please her right, I took her hand and led her in my bedroom that's never had a woman in it. I had to make sure we were in a place I could make love to her in and not just fuck. She backed up against the bed as I removed my slippers.

"You look real good T." I made my way to her.

"I wanna make sure you're satisfied." She sealed our lips with an intense and passionate kiss. It's nothing like the regular kissing we did. As our tongues collided on their own mission, I felt her small hands on the sides of my basketball shorts. She sucked on my bottom lip and had me step outta them.

"I want you Shak." I didn't get a chance to respond because her tongue began trailing down my body. I've never had a woman take her time tryna please me so this shit was driving me insane.

I felt her grab the base of my dick and direct it to her awaiting mouth. She opened up wide and slid her tongue over the top before deep throating me. My ass was so lost in the pleasure I had to hold on to the dresser to keep from falling. My knees were becoming weaker and my dick began twitching. I thought she'd get up but the moment I came and she suctioned all my seeds out like a vacuum, I knew then she could never be with another man. Ain't no way in hell I'm allowing her to make someone feel this got damn good.

"You ok." She swirled her tongue over the tip again before kissing it and standing up.

"I'm good but it's your turn."

"You damn right it is." She gestured with her finger as she backed up against the bed.

I turned her around, unzipped the outfit and let it fall to the ground. Teri has a bad ass body and knowing I'm about to be the last man to enter it, gave me a sense of entitlement. I felt like from here on out, no one should even speak to her. I know how my cousins feel about their women and thought about the many times they mentioned me falling for someone.

Mazza said, I'll know because she'll be the only one I wake up and go to bed thinking about. Fazza on the other hand said, it depends on how she is in the bedroom and orally she's perfect. Shawn told me, conversation and how she interacts with people around you. So far, everything is what they say except the sex because we haven't engaged in it yet. I don't even think I'd care of it wasn't the best. As long as she's around it's the only thing that matters.

I bent her over, spread her ass cheeks, got on my knees and let my tongue run up and down from her pussy to her ass. She gripped the comforter and silently moaned out. Once I dove in, her silence turned into loud.

"Make me cum Shak." She lifted one leg on the bed and her pussy was wide open. I turned, and sat against the footboard. I had her put it on my face, pulled down harder and drew her nub in my mouth. I could hear her gasping as the powerful orgasm took control. I stuck my finger in her ass and pussy at the same time and her body collapsed. Her nectar was seeping out and covering my face. When her breathing slowed down, I stood behind her and in one push, thrusted myself inside and stopped.

"Ahhhhhhh fuck!" She shouted.

She was tight, warm and super wet. My chest was touching her back as I grabbed her hands and lifted them above her head.

"I'm ready to give you what you want Teri." I whispered in her ear.

"Shak."

"I'm all yours." I sucked on her neck leaving hickeys.

"Fuck me Shak."

"Not until you tell me you're mine."

"I'm all yours baby. Please give it to me." I twisted her body to look at me and placed a kiss on her lips.

I buried myself deeper and could tell she felt pain and pleasure by the expressions on her face. I roughly jerked her hair and pounded into her with no mercy. I wanted her to know there's no other man out here that's gonna do her as good.

I flipped her over, threw her legs over my shoulder and watched her experience an orgasm that had her eyes rolling, body shaking and digging in my chest. My hand went around her throat as I continued thrusting in and out.

"I want us Shak. Don't hurt me." The moment those words left her mouth, I slowed up and began making love to her. It's the only thing I waited to hear. I wanted to know she had the same intentions.

"Never. Come here." I took her hands in mine, lifted her up with us connected and placed her against the wall. Her pussy began writhing around me as she chased that orgasm. My fingers were digging in her ass holding and thrusting deeper.

"Oh shit T. I'm about to cum."

"Me too. Fuckkkkkkkk!" I emptied my seeds in her with no regrets. My mom wanted grandkids and she's gonna get them soon. My dick twitched until every seed left my body. I kissed her tenderly, let her down and saw my cum dripping down her leg.

"You did it on purpose." I smirked.

"And I'm gonna keep doing it." I carried her in the bathroom where we had more sex. Off and on all night, she let me fuck, then switch and make love. Yea, we belong together.

****

"I want you too ma. Don't play with my heart." She turned to me. After we took it there the other night, she said it to me but I never said it back.

"You've never been in love?" I put on the right blinker and turned down the street.

"No and I can't even tell you if it's what I feel for you but I know when you didn't wanna have anything to do with me, I was lost."

"You were." She smiled and ran her hand down my face.

"Yup." We both sat quiet. She was thinking about what I said and I was wondering if it is love I'm feeling.

"Don't make me kill you." I snapped my neck to see if she were serious and almost crashed.

"You ain't killing shit." I parked in front of the house and shut the car off.

"Don't underestimate me because I'm a woman. I have a dark side too."

"Yea a'ight. Let's go." I opened the door.

"Why are we here?" Her face was turned up.

"I told you I want us, therefore; changes have to be made. I mean if you want me to keep this place I will."

"You about to bring my dark side out. Don't play with me." I opened her door, and walked up with her hand in mine. It felt weird showing public affection but she had me in a place where I didn't care.

"This is nice babe." She glanced around and decided to give herself a tour.

"I know."

"What you doing here?" I asked Cheryl who moved out weeks ago.

"Tasha called asking me to get the rest of my things. When I got here they wanted sex and I'm over them. Women or not, I'm not cheating on him."

"He must be laying it down."

"Not better than you but he's pretty good." She went to leave and Teri came stepping in from off the deck.

"Well, look here. I'm happy for you Shak. Hi, I'm Cheryl and it's good to see you are able to calm him down." She held her hand out and Teri had no problem shaking it.

"Thank you I guess."

"Trust me. He's never ever brought a woman here or even had one out in public. Whatever you did made an impact."

"Bye Cheryl."

"What? Shit, I saw how upset you were hearing those two bitches lied to her." Teri glanced over at me with a smirk.

"Don't say shit." She put her hands up.

"Anyway, let me go see my man. He supposed to surprise me for my birthday."

"Happy Birthday." Teri and I called out at the same time.

"Shak baby, is that you?" I heard Barb's voice and witnessed Teri's facial expression.

"Well I'm gone. I don't wanna see their faces when you make them leave."

"How you know what I'm about to do?"

"Like I said. No woman is gonna be ok with this setup. Bye Teri. Nice to meet you." She waved and closed the door behind her.

"Yea I'm here. Come right in." I told my security on the phone.

"At least she's cool not fucking you anymore." Her arms were around my neck.

"Are you?"

"I don't have an issue with her. She respected my presence and I appreciate that."

"I can't wait to dig in that pussy again."

"And I can't wait for you to fill me up with this banging ass, long, thick and amazing dick. I love sucking on it too. Your cum taste real good."

"You play too much." I had her against the wall.

"You tryna fuck this trifling bitch in our house." Things got outta control just that fast. Teri moved outta my grip and started banging Barb's head in the wall. Tasha attempted to jump in. I gave her a look and she backed up.

"A'ight ma. She gets it." I pulled Teri off and Barb looked as if she were about to pass out.

"You let her fight me Shak?" I didn't even bother answering because it was a dumb question.

"You got ten minutes to get outta here."

"What?" Tasha shouted.

"You heard me. My woman ain't letting me keep a ho house so y'all gotta go."

"After all these years. Really?"

"I told all of you from the beginning if I ever had a main chick this would be over. Each of you were ok with it."

"Ten minutes ain't enough time to move." Tasha was crying but I don't know why. She had a job and saved her money like the other two.

"What? You need twenty or a half hour."

"How about 30 days?" Barb said and I glanced at Teri who didn't have one mark on her.

"Eight minutes left bitch. Hurry the fuck up or I'ma drag you out." I chuckled at her being petty. Tasha hauled ass upstairs and Barb took her time.

"What you need boss?" Security came in with a couple of guys.

"Those bitches have seven minutes left to gather their things. If they're not finished, toss them out and lock up. This house is officially on the market."

"You got it. Hey Teri." They all spoke to her. It's only been a few days of me showcasing her and everyone seems to approve. I just had to let her meet the family, which is where we going now.

"I'm gonna miss this place." I said in the car before pulling off.

"Don't make me fuck you up Shak." I busted out laughing and went to the next destination.

"Am I dressed ok?" C asked for the fourth time. We were on our way to my grandparents' house. They are hell bent on meeting the new woman in my life. Anyone who kept me away from Kim is fine with them.

"You're perfect. But..." I parked and saw Shak pulling in.

"But what?" I helped her out and leaned her against the truck.

"If you think my cousins are bad, wait til you meet their father. He's a twin too but his brother isn't as bad. The women will love you and so will my grandfather."

"Your grandfather?"

"Yea, he's a big ass pervert." Her eyes got big as hell but it's the truth. She needs to prepare herself for him.

"My father is a different story." I took her hand in mine and walked over to Shak.

"He's gonna ask for grandkids." She busted out laughing.

"What up?" Shak walked over holding Teri's hand. I was happy he found someone because he was sticking his dick everywhere. His mom thought he'd catch a disease.

"Teri did you stop holding your coochie hostage?" Her sister sucked her teeth.

"I'm just asking because there's a few hickeys on your neck and you're with him." The two of them hadn't really spoken because she's been with me and when she wasn't, it was all about the new building.

I stayed with her and her mom in the building as they picked out furniture, had the electric, cable and whatever else turned on. Yea, she wanted a 50 inch in her and Teri's office. The conference, staff room and lobby all needed them with stereo surround. The people from Best Buy cane and hung them on the wall too. She had a huge water fountain that lit up in the middle of the lobby as well as chairs and tables for magazines. The furniture, desks, copier and other office equipment will be in during the week.

I was extremely proud of her and after months of being together, I made plans to be in her life for a very long time.

She's smart, corny, loveable and about her money. Women can say what they want, but they'll never call her stupid or broke that's for sure.

I also admired her for getting back to work after suffering the death of her son. She and I both go there two or three times a week, even if it's just to say hi or put flowers on the graves. It's sad because I've been asking the people who work there if anyone else goes and besides her and her family, the punk doesn't. He may go late at night but I doubt it. I'm glad he messed up because she fell right in my lap; literally.

"Grams, where you at?" I yelled and Shak went to introduce Teri to his uncle, who is my grandfather. I can't even imagine what he's about to say.

"Hey honey. Is this her?" She walked around C.

"Hi. I'm C'Yani. It's a pleasure to meet you." She held her hand out for my grandmother to shake.

"It's nice to meet you two. You're very pretty." C started blushing.

"Let me see if my grandson got him a sexy chick like my great nephew." I heard him before he even stepped in the kitchen.

"GOT DAMN SHE BAD. I don't know which one to stare at. Whew! Y'all picked some good ones." He licked his lips and C backed into me.

"He's a horn dog but he won't touch you. My grandmother has him scared."

"If my grandson ain't hitting it right, his pop pop will surely help him out."

"That's inappropriate." C said and everyone stopped to look.

"What's inappropriate are these tight jeans that look painted on. And this shirt has your titties damn near coming out. I bet if I stand over you, I can see straight down your shirt." She sucked her teeth.

"Did you say he was a reverend?"

"A nasty one." I whispered in her ear.

"Well I'm not appreciating the way he's speaking to me. He and I have nothing to discuss, therefore; this will be my last visit." The entire room erupted in laughter.

"Honey, just say don't talk to me like that or beat it." My grandmother told her. She's not ignorant to his flirty and inappropriate ways.

"Yo, how you get a corny girl?" Fazza asked coming in the room with Ty behind him. He was about to start fucking with her and we all knew it.

"Excuse me. I am not corny." She had her hands on her hips.

"Are you black?"

"Fazza leave her alone." Ty stood in front of him and introduced herself.

"I'm just asking because maybe she doesn't know."

"How in the hell wouldn't she know?"

"Her skin is brown, and she has nappy hair but the way she's acting makes me think she doesn't know." He went to touch it and I moved her away. My girl's hair is not nappy but Fazza said every woman's hair is if she's black.

"What? I'm just saying. She talks proper and seems to be stuck up. Most women like that don't know."

"FAZZA!" All the women shouted.

"I am black sir and I don't think you should be questioning my background. I could've easily interpreted you as a ghetto nigga off the street who had no home training but I didn't."

"Girl, calm your corny ass down. I'm only fucking with you. But I do want you to remind yourself when around hood people, that you are black. Learn our lingo sister." He put his fist up like black power and Ty pushed him in the other room.

"Don't worry about it. I'll make you feel better later."

"I hope so because it's gonna be a long day and I need to release some frustration." I started cracking up. I loved the way she spoke.

"Are all the men rude?"

"Yup. What up C?" Lil Faz gave her a hug.

"I have to get used to this."

"If you plan on being with his ugly ass you do."

"Hey. I happen to find him very sexy and attractive."

"That's because he turned your corny ass out." He and I both started laughing.

"Meekkkkk!" She whined.

"Come on. Let me introduce you to my dad."

"I don't know if I want to."

"You'll be fine." I put her on my shoulder like a kid and went to the family room where I knew he'd be. His feet were up in the recliner and he was debating something on television with Mazza, Shak's stepdad and my grandfather.

"Pops, I want you to meet C'Yani." He turned and smiled.

"C'Yani Bailey. It's good to see you again." He stood and gave her a hug.

"You know this white woman?" Fazza had me cracking up. When C'Yani looked at me, I stopped. I can say something but she doesn't seem to be too upset.

"She ain't white nigga. She just don't talk ignorant like yo ass. Now leave my future daughter in law alone."

"Ughhhh."

"Daughter in law? Pops it's way too early."

"When you told me about a guy you met who swept you off your feet, I had no idea it was my son." She gave him a look to be quiet.

"How you know each other?"

"I've been working with her for a year. Duh, she's the one who I hired to do your advertising."

"Hold up."

"I didn't know babe. I know it's Gibson construction but I didn't put two and two together."

"Yup she's white. The ditzy white girl." C walked over to Fazza and stood in front of him.

"You're gonna stop talking shit to me, or me and your wife are gonna whoop your ass. Now fuck with it if you want." She rolled her neck and everything. Ty was hysterical and so were all the women.

"I don't know why you laughing Ty because that pussy gonna be real sore since you wanna be on her side." She gave him the finger and walked to my girl.

"I'm proud of you C. Welcome to the family." Zia and Ty took her in the kitchen with the other women.

"Leave my girl alone."

"Nigga you should've said that in the beginning like Shakim did. I like his girl though. She's feisty."

"C, is just what I need and I don't want yo ass scaring her away."

"Shut yo ass up." He and I started wrestling and then Shakim and Mazza started. All of us were going back and forth. Some of the young kids jumped in too.

"If y'all don't get your grown asses out my house with that shit, I'm shooting all y'all." My grandmother was no joke so when she said it, we all went out in the back. It wasn't too cold but we needed jackets.

After we all ate and sat around talking shit, everyone started leaving. We had to work the next day anyway. The twin's wives loved Teri and C and made plans to stay in touch and go out. I had no problem with it because my family is close. I expect any new additions to be the same.

****

"You coming in?"

"I gotta get up early but if you want me here I'll stay."

224

"No it's ok. I did want to release some stress but I can wait until tomorrow." She leaned over to kiss me.

"Let me get some clothes and I'll be back."

"I'll be waiting for you."

"Have on one of those sexy outfits."

"Maybe." She opened the door.

"Maybe nothing. It's either that or be naked."

"I'll surprise you." She pecked my lips and I watched her go in. Once the door closed, I pulled off to go grab my things.

"What up?" I answered through Bluetooth. I figured it was Shak because we were talking at the house about returning to Connecticut. He wanted to get those dudes and get it out the way. Evidently, they've been popping a lotta shit and made plans to return.

"What's up is you paying me to remain quiet but a good dick down will do." Jasmine spoke in the phone. I hung up and she called back. Instead of answering, I made a detour to her crib. I hopped out with my truck still running and kicked the door down.

"What... I was just playing..." She looked terrified.

"Now you playing right?" I had her pressed against the wall. Her face was to the side and my chest was almost touching her back.

"You got one more time to threaten me and I swear your head is gonna show up on your momma's porch detached from your body." I banged her head into the wall a few times and watched her body drop.

"You fucking with the wrong nigga." I walked out and jumped back in my ride.

"Hey baby." I didn't notice Kim in the passenger seat. Where did she come from?

"Get the fuck out."

"Not until we rekindle our love. Meek, YOU KNOW HOW MUCH I LOVE YOU." She shouted and I pulled off. I went on the highway to get home, reached over and pretended to rub her leg. I opened the door and pushed her stupid ass out. I looked in my rear-view mirror and she was lying in the middle of the street. Good riddance. I hope somebody runs over her. Let me hurry up and get to C. I definitely need to

fuck this stress away. *Crazy ass bitches.*

"Keep sucking. Here I cum C'Yani. Ahh shit." I came extremely hard and opened my eye to see Jasmine standing there with an attitude. I don't even know why I called out her name when she doesn't even go down on me.

"I'm sorry Jas. This stuff with C'Yani and the gangster dude is really getting to me." She stormed off and I heard the bathroom door slam. I thought about knocking but she needed time to cool off. Calling another woman's name is messed up; especially during sex.

As I laid there the doorbell rang. Jas walked in the room looking at me.

"You expecting someone?" Both of us went to the window. I panicked after seeing who was here.

"Oh shit. Go in the guest room." I pushed her out the way and down the hall.

"Why am I hiding Ty? Or should I say, why are we hiding? Who cares if she knows we're together?"

"Can you do what I ask?" The doorbell rang again.

"Ty this is..."

228

"I'll buy you whatever."

"A new house?"

"Yea whatever." She backed in with a grin on her face.

"If you make one sound, you're not getting one."

"Alright damn." She rolled her eyes as I closed the door and ran down the steps to open the other one.

"C'Yani. What are you doing here?"

"I wanted to drop your things off." I stared at the three huge totes on the side of her car.

"You didn't have to do that."

"Actually, I did. The house finally sold and I had to get rid of everything." I noticed her eyes becoming watery.

"I miss him too."

WHAP! She smacked me so hard I swore stars floated around my head.

"Bitch are you crazy?" I pushed her against the wall of my house.

"Get your dirty pathetic hands off me." She tried to move me back but I had a grip on her hair and shirt.

"You smack me and tell me not to touch you?"

229

"How dare you mention missing my son and you haven't even been to his grave? Let's not forget you were too busy having sex with another woman to even answer your phone." I loosened my grip and let go.

"I apologized for that C'Yani but you act like he was in my stomach. You're the one who stressed yourself out, wouldn't eat and the reason he died." Her mouth hit the floor and tears flooded her eyes.

"I didn't mean it. Shit." She slid outta my grip that loosened up and had her knees to her chest, crying hysterical.

"Leave me alone Ty."

"C'Yani, I'm sorry." She shook her head back and forth.

"How could you Ty?"

"How could I what?"

"I thought you loved me. How could you cheat on me?"

"Not this again. C'Yani, I said I was sorry and wanted to start over but you're with that thug." She ignored the mention of her little boyfriend.

"I know the sex wasn't perfect but if you took the time to sit me down we could've gone to therapy or something." I

230

put my head down because she's right. Everything in the relationship was perfect except the sex. I mentioned it but didn't dwell on it, which is why I stepped out.

"I still love you C'Yani." I moved her hands, lifted her face and kissed her deeply.

"What are you doing?" She pushed me off.

"I have a man now and..."

"I don't care about him. We've been together too long for you to write me off like I don't mean shit."

"Oh, like you did to her." I turned and there stood the same humongous dude from before. He had another guy with him and both of them didn't appear to be happy.

"Meek, what are you doing here? Not that I mind." She stood and walked over to him.

"You told me on the phone you'd call me back in two minutes. When you didn't, I knew something wasn't right. Why are you crying?" Damn this nigga had to be in love or something.

"He said some hurtful things to me and..." My entire body hit the floor and I felt something cold on the side of my face.

"You're lucky she asked me not to kill you because I've been wanting to for weeks now." I didn't say anything.

"She was being nice and brought your things even after I told her to toss them. The least you could've done is appreciated the gesture and not talk shit."

"Baby, I'm ready to go."

"I'll meet you at the house." I heard a car door close and it pull off.

"Like I was saying. One more time and I'm gonna murk you and that stupid bitch you hiding upstairs." My face had to be bleeding because he slammed the butt of the gun down on it hard. How the hell did he know Jasmine is here?

"Over here talking shit and you probably just finished fucking her." He put the gun in his waist.

"And tell that bitch stop playing with me or she's next." He kicked me hard in the ribs and went to his truck. How in the hell did my ex end up with a guy like him?

"JASMINE!" I shouted and limped in the kitchen.

"What happened to you?"

"The man C'Yani is seeing stopped by and left a message for the two of us."

"A message?" She grabbed some ice out the kitchen and placed a bunch of paper towels on my face.

"We better leave them alone or else."

"Or else what?" I gave her a look.

"I'm just asking."

"Well don't ask questions we both know the answers to. I can't believe how happy they seem to be." I didn't see them showing a lot of affection but you could tell he had deep feelings for her. Then, she called him baby and told her he'd see her at the house. Are they sleeping together?

"Let's come up with a plan to break them up."

"We can't beat him and she didn't do anything."

"No but you kissed her and he's been to my house."

"I don't know Jas."

"Don't worry. I got this." She pecked my lips and helped me clean up.

"What happened to your face?" My mom barked and lifted the bandage. After Jasmine cleaned me up, I had her drive to the emergency room and thankfully I went because I needed six stitches.

"C'Yani dropped by last week to bring me my things. I said hurtful stuff, kissed her and then the big, bad boyfriend came to her rescue but not without warning me."

"Warning you?" I sat at the table and watched as she poured me some iced tea.

"He told me to leave her alone and that me or Jasmine better not test him. You know the normal things thugs say." I may not be in the streets but I'm also not naive to a man threatening me. If he can bust my face open with a gun, I can't imagine the other things he'd do.

"Thug?"

"Yup. She has a street guy."

"Well if he's treating her good, I'm all for it."

"Really ma?" She sat across from me.

234

"Son, that woman loved you down to your dirty draws. So what if she wasn't a freak in the bedroom. You should've worked it out instead of shacking up with some whore." I sucked my teeth.

"I know it's hard to hear but she's suffered a lot and deserves to be happy."

"But a thug?"

"Her choice hun, just like it was yours to look elsewhere for sex. Let that woman be."

"I still love her."

"And she'll always love you but it's time to move on." I fell back in the chair staring at the ceiling. Could I let her go?

"That woman is here again." Mia spoke with heavy sarcasm this time. I looked up, saw the way she rolled her eyes and pressed the intercom for security to come up. I had no idea who she spoke of because again, different people, men and women came through these doors daily.

"Yes Mr. Gibson." Two of the men stood next to Mia who appeared to be nervous.

"Mia here, seems to be overworked. She's going to be taken off the schedule for ten days and if I feel she should return, I'll inform you. Until then, strip her of the company's badge, cell phone, and have tech support come in to change the information on her computer."

"Mr. Gibson, I'm sorry." I stood, fixed my pants and walked over to her.

"I told you over and over this is a place of business and the individuals who enter these doors are all clients or potentials. You can't seem to separate whatever ill feelings you have toward them, therefore; you need time off." She started crying.

"She is not to reenter unless you hear directly from me. Am I understood?"

"Yes sir."

"Please let me stay. It won't happen again."

"The problem is, I gave you too many chances in which it made you believe nothing would happen. I'll have HR contact you in ten days if I have you return." Security stood behind her as she gathered her things and I glanced around to see who she spoke of because no one was sitting there. Then I saw her coming out the bathroom and smiled. C'Yani had a way of making my heart skip a beat.

She had a huge bag on her shoulder and the dressed down look is cute. The jeans were fitted, her coat was opened so I could see the sweater and her calf boots had a small heel on them. I'm used to her wearing business attire during the week so this is new to me.

"Hey sexy." She blushed like always.

"Jennifer, can I see you in my office?" I removed the bag off C's shoulder, grabbed her hand and stepped in.

"I like seeing you this way." I sat the bag down and pulled her on my lap in the chair.

"It's pretty comfortable and I like seeing you in this." She lifted my tie. We heard someone clear their throat.

"I apologize. This is inappropriate."

"Girl bye. I'm happy he found someone; shit we all are. He isn't as grouchy." Jennifer closed the door, took a seat across from me and prepared herself to take notes.

"Really?"

"Yes. Before you, no one really spoke in the office on the days he came. I'm assuming it's been a few months, right?" C nodded.

"A'ight. Don't be tryna play me." She waved me off and told C she loved the boots.

"I'm gonna sit over here." She went over to the couch and took her phone out.

"I like her for you Meek." Jennifer is my office manager and has been here since I first opened. She's cool as hell and always took initiative if I weren't here to make sure shit ran right. Being an office manager is one thing but sometimes she had to play HR, and a few other positions. I appreciated the hell outta her and she's compensated well.

"Yea. She's my calm that's for sure." I smiled looking at her type away on her phone. She constantly answered emails whenever we were out. Sometimes I had to take the phone from her just to get her attention.

"Is she stuck up?" I chuckled.

"Very but not in an ignorant way."

"How is that?"

"She's high maintenance because her parents have her that way, yet; she's down to earth in a corny sense. She'll give you the clothes off her back and expect nothing in return. And, she's been doing her thing in starting her own business."

"You love her."

"This is what I need you to do." I ignored her question because honestly, I didn't know if it were love. We're together all the time and I'm definitely feeling her but I'm not sure. She noticed me ignore her and continued with her own questions.

"Ok. Do you want me to hire through a temp agency for the ten days?"

"Nah. I want you to take her spot and I'll pay you."

"Hell yea, you will." She laughed and stood to leave.

"Nice meeting you C'Yani and please keep him happy."

"I'll try." I told Jen to lock the door and gestured for C to come close. She unzipped the calf boots, took them off and stood.

"I'm assuming she gave me the stamp of approval." She lifted the sweater over her head and threw it on the chair.

"As long as you have mine nothing else matters." I grabbed my dick when she removed her jeans.

"Do I have yours?" She kneeled in front of me, had me sit up to get my pants and boxers down and looked at me.

"I've never been into oral sex but I absolutely love sucking your dick and allowing you to cum in my mouth." No idea why the corny line turned me on so much but it did and my man jumped.

"Take care of your man C." She smiled.

"I am." Her mouth opened and I watched as she took me to ecstasy in no time.

"Let me help you out." I lifted her up and fumbled with the bra a little. Her breasts fell free and she pushed my face into her chest. I pulled one of her nipples in my mouth and swirled my tongue over it. Her body began to quiver.

"I love the way you make me feel Meek." Her head fell back as I continued sucking. I removed those thin panties, and had her sit on the window sill. No one could see this high up.

I pulled the chair over, opened her legs and smiled at the sight before me. Her hands went to the side as she attempted to make herself comfortable. I now had her vulnerable with her pussy in my face. My arms went around her hips as I allowed my tongue to press against her overgrown nub. I licked and sucked on her entire pussy and a few times made it down to her ass. Her taste was addicting and I wanted and needed more.

"Oh fuckkkk Meek." She reached for my dreads and pushed her hips forward onto my face and succumbed to the first orgasm. I allowed her to reach another one before placing myself in between.

"You like the way we fuck C?" She nodded and kissed me feverishly. I slid inside and felt her walls close down on me.

"Yesssss baby. I love it." She sucked on my neck and grinded her pussy into me. Our pelvises were moving to their own beat and neither of us cared to stop.

"Fuck me harder Meek." I smiled, lifted her in my arms and fucked the shit outta her. My nut began to build and the pressure to let go was right there.

"You ready?"

"Yes. I need it."

"I'm cumming C." She continuously bit in my shoulder to keep the moans down from her orgasm but nothing prepared me for what she said next.

"I love you Mekhi Gibson." Her head was on my shoulder as I sat in the chair with her still connected.

"Let me wash you up." She nodded and I took her in the bathroom. The whole time I thought of her comment, yet; couldn't respond. My feelings ran deep like I said before but I had to make sure it's love and not lust.

242

After the two of us got dressed, she brought the bag over to me and opened it up. There was food, chips and drinks in there. Once again, I couldn't understand why her ex did bad shit to her. I'm not saying she is repeating whatever they did but still. C, is a great woman and any man would be lucky to have her.

"I picked you up a sub because I didn't know what you wanted."

"I ate already." I sat her on my lap and started laughing.

"You're nasty. Here." She opened the chips and fed me a few.

"I would feed you the sandwich but it's nasty to touch on someone's food."

"Anything I have, you can touch."

"Do you love me Meek? Wait! Is it too early for me to tell you?" I turned her to face me.

"It's never too early to reveal how you feel. As far as me loving you, I don't know." I felt her body tense up.

"I'm not saying it won't happen but I do know my feelings run very deep."

243

"Not deep enough to love me?"

"C, I'm not gonna tell you what you wanna hear if it's not how I'm feeling. I don't want you upset or assuming I should be in love if you are."

"No. I get it." She slammed the chips on the table and started to get her things.

"C'Yani."

"I have things to do." She was angry and I hated that. We've never had an argument and I never wanted to see her upset.

"C. Stop." I grabbed her arm when she zipped her boot up.

"I get it Meek. You're not in love and you're scared and nervous because of what your ex did. You're unsure of what you feel and even though I'm in love with you, you refuse to be forced to reveal things you may not feel. Right?" She had her hands on her hips.

"Well yea but..."

"No need to respond with something that may frustrate me even more. I'll see you around."

"Wait! You breaking up with me?" She walked up and put her hand on my face.

"Meek, I'm in love with you. This isn't infatuation or lust for me. It's the real thing but what I'm not going to do, is sit around hoping and praying one day you realize its love and not lust. I don't want to waste time on someone who doesn't know what he wants."

"I didn't say that."

"I know Meek and I'm not trying to confuse you or portray myself as a crazy woman. However; you know the exact type of woman I am and I've never lied to you. But it's best if we go our separate ways now to avoid any hurt. I'll see you around." She picked her stuff up, opened the door and left me standing there stuck. *What the fuck just happened?*

"What did you do?" Jen stepped in with her arms folded.

"Nothing Why?" I sat in my chair.

"Her being upset doesn't seem like nothing." I explained and she agreed with C.

"She's not forcing you to respond Meek but I understand where she's coming from. Men waste time playing games and not trying to admit to love. I'm not saying you are but since you're unsure, she doesn't want to waste time when there's other men out there."

"Too bad she won't be with another man."

"Just like a man to become territorial over a woman he can't let go."

"What the fuck ever." She stood.

"She's not going to allow you anymore access in her world until you're sure Meek." She placed her hand on my arm.

"If you can't give her what she wants, then let her be. She's a good woman from what you say and needs a man who sees a future with them and not an unsure one." She kissed my cheek and walked out. I sat there tryna decide if I should go after her or leave her alone. Whatever the case, she still won't sleep with another man. I don't care what anyone says.

I was devastated leaving Meeks office. Of course, I
didn't expect him to relay those three words to me because I
did. However; I refuse to waste another five years putting my
all into a relationship with a man who's unsure if he'll ever be
in love.

I made sure not to give him an ultimatum but let him
know where I stood. For God's sake, I'm having sex with this
man and at any time he could sleep with someone else.

In the beginning with Ty, we were deep in love with
one another. Sex wasn't an issue until two years ago but it's
also when he began to change. He began frequenting bars more
and wanting to perform different sexual acts. I always assumed
it to be the liquor making him that way but come to find out,
it's how he felt. I should've listened and gave in but I couldn't.
He didn't make me comfortable during sex like Meek did.

Anyway, once he started cheating I knew he could no
longer be in love. In my eyes, a man in love will never allow
any woman to disrupt or disrespect their relationship. He took

this woman on vacations, purchased her expensive things and basically treated her like his number one.

I couldn't believe he saw nothing wrong and felt it was ok to do it. I made it no better by ignoring the evidence placed in my face. I don't blame him for everything because in the end, I stayed. It's the exact reason I refused to allow years to pass me by again. Meek and I have been a couple for six months now and if he isn't in love or even love me, why waste time?

"C, you can't expect him to say it because you did." Teri said in the kitchen as I pulled the manicotti out. I loved cooking. She finished making the salad and sat in on the table. We had dinner together a lot.

"I know which is why I walked away. I don't want to pressure him and I'm protecting my heart. Yes, I'm in love with him and it's gonna hurt for a while but it's nothing I can do."

"I guess."

"Yo! What you cook C?" Shak busted in the house with his evil ass cousins behind him. I peeked to see if Meek were here. When Teri mentioned she gave him a key. I knew she was in love too.

"He's not here sis relax." Shak sat down and put Teri on his lap. I loved the way she got him to settle down. If I didn't know any better, I'd definitely say they were going to get married.

"He's probably fucking some new chick to get over you." Lil Faz said and I tossed the dish rag at him.

"I bet you don't eat." I told him and made a plate for Mystic. I always made extra because we usually took dinner for lunch the next day.

"I bet you don't either." He stood over me looking at the biscuits I pulled out.

"How you figure?"

"Because once your plate is filled up, I'm knocking it out your hand. If I don't eat, neither do you."

"That's very rude."

"You already know what it is. Try me." He gave me a sneaky grin and even if I wanted to, I didn't. My ass is hungry as hell.

"Anyway, Mystic how's basketball?" He was the brother who had prospects watching him already.

"Good. When you taking my cousin out the dog house?" He asked and they all stared at me.

"He's not in the dog house. We chose to go in different directions." I handed him and lil Faz a plate.

"Yea right."

"What."

"Let that nigga hear another man visiting and watch this house catch on fire or something." Mystic thought he was hilarious telling me that and so did lil Faz and Shak.

"It's not that serious."

"Not to you but he likes your corny ass ex. It's not over until he says so." I glanced at Teri and she had nothing to say.

"Don't look at her. I wish the fuck she would have another man here."

"Nigga you don't own me."

"I own this pussy so what's the need in having male company? He ain't getting none. Fuck you talking about?" Shak began to get upset.

"Who raised you because your manners are horrible?"

"My cousins, mother and stepfather."

"Besides your mom I can see why you are this way."

"Don't come for my pops Teri. He likes you." Mystic said and mushed her.

"I know but I need my man to be gentle sometimes." He leaned Teri back and kissed her.

"I'm gentle when I'm in that pussy." She snickered like a kid. All of us shook our heads. Those two stay arguing but you couldn't tell they weren't in love.

"Don't nobody wanna hear that shit." Mystic mushed him in the head and they ran in the living room to wrestle. What is it with them and wrestling? Lil Faz ain't move and said he's finishing his food. Afterwards, we all sat in the living room watching a movie when the doorbell rang. Mystic went to answer it.

"Is C'Yani Bailey here?" All of us looked.

"Who the fuck are you?" Teri barked at the familiar woman. How the hell did she know where I lived?

251

"Can we speak in private?" Mia asked and Mystic was now breathing down her neck.

"I'm not sure why you're here but showing up unannounced is not appreciated. Whatever you need to say, can be done in front of everyone."

"Yo, Meek know you here?" Shak barked and began walking towards her. I guess he knows who she is.

"No. I just wanted to ask her if she could get him, to give me my job back."

"So you show up at her fucking house?" Everyone was digging in her ass.

"Look Mia. I don't know the relationship the two of you share or shared; nor do I care. I'm not the reason you were suspended. Your attitude, bad choice of words and the way you introduce potential clients to a businessman did it."

"You think you're better than me?"

"Oh hell no." Teri was pissed and Shak already had Mia by the waist throwing her out.

"IT WON'T LAST BITCH. HE'LL NEVER LOVE YOU THE WAY HE LOVES HER. YOU'RE NOT WOMAN

ENOUGH FOR HIM YOU STUPID BITCH. I HOPE MY SISTER FINDS AND KILLS YOU."

"Your sister?" Teri and I both asked, as Shak tossed her in the car.

"Don't you worry. I gave her this address so expect the unexpected."

POW! Mystic shot the back window out her car and lil Faz let off some shots too. I covered my mouth because I've never seen anything like it.

"Fuck her C. Meek ain't gonna let anything happen to you." Shak had me go inside but I couldn't help but wonder if it's any truth to her rant. Would her sister come after me and who the hell is she?

****

"You're telling me this woman showed up at your house and threatened you with her sister?" My mom asked as the men brought in more furniture for the lobby of my new building. It's been a couple of months since I started the process of opening my own firm and its coming along perfect.

253

Teri had been by decorating her floor as well for the Accounting firm she was opening. Her and Jasmine have been here nonstop and each time we pass one another, a chill goes down my spine. Something is off with her and I hate she even has to be here but Teri's her friend. I can't tell her not to allow her here. I mean, I can since I'm the owner of the building but I'm not like that. If she gets outta hand it's a different story.

"Yea. Thank goodness Shak and his cousins were there. I mean she was hysterical yelling about Meek. Do you think she slept with him too?"

"I doubt it. A woman throwing out things like that would've already told. Make sure you stay away from her."

"You don't have to worry about that." My mom put her hands on my shoulder.

"C'Yani she sounds like a crazy woman and obviously her sister ain't too far. Promise you'll run the other way and call the cops if you see her." She had a serious look on her face.

"I promise."

"Ok. I've seen too many movies and women on the news who think they can handle themselves and the situation gets out of control. I don't want anything bad to happen."

"Hello ladies." We turned around and Jasmine stood there.

"Hey honey. What did you do to your hair? I like. It's the same color as yours C'Yani." My mom gave her a hug.

"Why would you have your hair color changed?"

"You're not the only one who can have this color C'Yani. Anyway, I'm so excited for the grand opening."

"Why are you excited? You don't have an office here." I folded my arms and she smiled.

"Actually, Teri said I could use an office here for clients. You know I have my license and never used it. She's my best friend, so why not?"

"That's great Jasmine. All of you will be working here together."

"Yea, perfect. Will you two excuse me?"

"What's wrong with her?" She asked my mother but I didn't hear the response. I walked down the steps and to Teri's office. I went passed the secretaries desk and all the cubicles to the back where her personal office is. The door was closed and you could hear music playing.

"TERI!" I banged on the door.

"Right there Shak. Yea baby." I heard her moan and my face became flushed.

"TERI OPEN THIS DOOR!" I wasn't trying to interrupt but we needed to talk.

"She'll be upstairs in a few C." Shak yelled out and I stormed to my office and paced the floor. There's no way this she can work here. Why did Teri even allow her without asking?

"You ok sweetie?" My mom closed the door.

"Jasmine can't work here."

"Why not? Her and Teri are friends and…"

"I don't trust her ma and she and I barely speak. Why would she want to work somewhere with a person she doesn't like?"

"Calm down C'Yani. Look at it this way. She has to pay rent therefore; even though you own the building, you'll make income off her and the vendors coming in."

"I don't want her money." She looked at the time on her phone.

"Ok. I have to pick your brother up from day care. Talk to Teri and see what's going on. Maybe she doesn't know how much you really don't care for her." I nodded and walked her out. When I returned to my office Jasmine was sitting at my desk.

"Get out!"

"C'Yani why don't you like me?"

"I'm not going to tell you again to leave my office." She rose out my chair and came towards me. Besides her hair she had a familiar look to her. I don't know what it is but I don't like it and I'm sure she's doing all this for a reason.

"You really should watch the men you keep."

"Excuse me." She had a grin on her face and closed the door. Yea, she's not working here.

"She's gonna be mad." Shak joked about C'Yani being upset. He stopped by to see me and as usual, one thing led to another with us. Ever since we began sleeping together, its like we couldn't keep our hands off.

"I know but something had to be wrong for her to be banging the way she was." He handed me my shirt.

"Let's go see." He opened the door and Jasmine was standing there.

"What the fuck you standing outside the door for?"

"Shak." I touched his arm and he pushed past her with an attitude.

"Let's go see what your sister wanted." He pulled me away and remained quiet the rest of the way.

"Please don't tell me you slept with her." He stopped before we got to C'Yani's door and moved the hair out my face.

"I would never sleep with someone who..." He cut himself off.

"I've never slept with her and I told you from the very beginning she's sneaky. Something ain't right with her Teri."

258

"Her attitude sucks but she good peoples." He ignored me and opened the door to my sister's office. If my sister was white, her face would be beet red. That's how angry she looked.

"How dare you invite that woman to work here without notifying me first?" Shak stared at me.

"This is supposed to be our building. I didn't know each person I hired had to go through you." She came over to me.

"Don't talk that nonsense to me Teri. This is a building I purchased and I'd never question anything you do and you know it. However; you are fully aware she and I don't care for one another and now she's going to run a business outta here? I will not accept it. She has to go."

"Hold the fuck up T. I know damn well she ain't talking about the bitch downstairs."

"Why does everyone hate her, and the entire floor is mine so if I want her to open up her business then I can. She doesn't have to come up here, nor do you have to walk on that floor."

"So, if I want to see my sister I have to wait until we get home or if you come here?"

"If that's what you wanna do."

"T, you dead ass fucking wrong."

"I never thought my sister would pick a woman over me but you know what." She went to pick her things up.

"You do what you want because that floor is yours right?"

"Yup." I said it with my arms folded.

"Make sure you or your employee don't step one foot on this got damn floor and the grand opening will be for my business only."

"Really?"

"Really and I'm moving out."

"Moving out?" I saw Shak shaking his head.

"Yea, that's your house and I've never said a word about her coming by because it's yours. Here this is a building I brought and you don't care how I feel about a woman not liking me work here."

"C'Yani you're not going to like everyone you work with. Is this how you'll react?"

"No because I wouldn't hire anyone who didn't care for me or my sister. It's a nightmare waiting to happen, which is exactly what this is. But don't worry, as long as you have your friend here."

"FINE! Move out then."

"Already in the process. Now get the hell out of my office. I need to pack." Shak looked at her and smirked. I guess he got a kick outta how she spoke.

"Good riddance." We walked out, she locked her door and stormed off. Shak wasn't too far behind.

"Shakim! Where are you going?" He turned around with an evil face.

"You're helping out a bitch who can't stand your sister."

"What is the problem?"

"Why didn't you speak to C'Yani about it?" I didn't answer because there was no reason on why I didn't.

"Yes, she gave you free range to do whatever but it's no way in hell you should've agreed to hiring her. What if she did some shit like that to you? Huh? Not only that, she couldn't wait to rub it in her face." I couldn't say a word because everything he was saying is true.

"That bitch is up to something and whether you sit in denial or not, it's going to somehow hurt your sister in the long run but all you seem to worry about is being a boss."

"Excuse me."

"C'Yani purchased this building for you and her. The only reason your name isn't on the paperwork is because you weren't there when she signed it. But you're so fucking hell bent on pleasing Jasmine, that you shitted all over C. You that desperate to be in charge?"

"I can buy my own building Shakim. My sister isn't the only one with money."

"You're not listening." He stood in my face.

"Who the fuck cares about the money? She did this for y'all." He started to walk away and turned around.

"In my eyes you have no loyalty and I can't be with a bitch like that."

"I'm a bitch now?"

"Yup because only dumb bitches do shit like you. We all know Jasmine can't stand your sister for some reason and we haven't even known you that long. Yet, you sit around and let her disrespect C on a regular and brush it off like it's her being funny."

"She doesn't have any real problems with my sister." He shook his head.

"The bitch don't like C'Yani for whatever reason and now you're forcing your sister to be uncomfortable in her place of work. What type of shit you on?"

"Shakim, don't leave." He chuckled and stared at Jasmine standing at the door. Where did she come from?

"You need to figure out your life because as long as she's in it, you're about to lose a lot more people than me and your sister. Tha fuck your stupid ass looking at?" He mushed her so hard she fell back and I heard her hit the ground.

"Shakim."

"I wish you would say something." I kept my mouth closed and followed him down the steps and out the door.

"Shak wait!"

"Wait for what Teri?"

"I don't want you to leave."

"Too bad. I suggest you make amends with your sister because that sneaky bitch has something up her sleeve." He hopped in his car and sped out the parking lot. I thought about following him and changed my mind.

The things he said hurt me and I couldn't help but wonder if what he said is true? Could Jasmine be planning to hurt my sister? I turned and looked at her getting off the floor. Nah, she ain't crazy.

****

"How have you been Teri?" I turned around and stared in the face of my ex Brian. I must admit he was still fine as hell and I couldn't erase the smile plastered on my face.

"I'm fine. How are you?" This is the first time I responded to him. I usually walk past but he caught me eating in the food court. Unless I'm tossing my food, I may as well respond.

"You look fine. I miss you." I put my head down.

"Look at me." He tilted my face.

"You don't feel the same?"

"I did until someone filled your spot."

"Teri, I never wanted you to leave but I understand why you did it. Just know I'll never stop loving you."

"If you told me this months ago, I probably would've asked if we could go to a room and make up for lost time. However; he came in at the right time and picked me up. I love everything about him." I noticed Shak standing there after those words left my mouth. We hadn't seen or spoken to one another since he left me at the job not too long ago.

"You don't love me anymore?"

"She said no. What part of that don't you understand?" Shakim stood in front of him with his two cousins he's always with. How the hell is Mystic even in school if he's always here? I stood to throw my food out and leave. Shakim looked hella good and I wanted to fuck him all night. Knowing it wouldn't happen I decided to go home.

"I should've known you'd find a street thug."

"Excuse me." I let the tray fall out my hand and heard it slam on the table.

"I was too white for you right?" I pushed Shakim out the way since he stood toe to toe with him. I saw his fists balled up and knew one hit would knock Brian out.

"I was in love with you Brian but there's no way you felt the same because if you did, it would've never been an issue standing up for me. Hell, I protected you from your family more than you did. Why would I stay with a man scared to put his parents in their place about the foul shit they did and said to his woman."

"Teri."

"Don't you dare try and make me feel like shit for leaving a bad situation." I grabbed my stuff and went to storm off only to be stopped by this crazy bitch.

"I told you to leave him alone, didn't I?"

"Barb what the fuck you doing?" I heard Shakim yell behind me, as I pushed past her.

Beep! Beep! I hit the alarm on my car and sat down. I closed the door and Barb stood there smirking. I tried to open the door to get out and ask why she was watching me and it wouldn't budge.

"What the hell?"

Outta nowhere the smell of gas engulfed my car. I could see Shakim walking in my direction. I started banging on the window and saw people running over to try and open it. Something was terribly wrong. I stared down at my phone to see my mom calling. I tried to answer but the smell overwhelmed me. I began coughing and my eyes were burning.

"TERIIIIII!" Shakim and the guys started banging on the window and pulling on the door handle. Tears streamed down my face as the darkness took over. I definitely didn't think I'd die this way.

"A table for one please." I came here to get away from the BS with my sister and Meek. It seems like pain followed wherever I went and the times I ate here, were extremely peaceful.

"Right this way." The woman smiled and sat me in the exact spot Meek and I did. He must not be coming if the table is free.

"Can I start you with a drink?" I told her what I wanted and asked for the crab nachos and stuffed mushrooms for an appetizer.

She left me alone and I began staring out the window. The waves were crashing against the rocks and some men were actually surfing in this weather. It wasn't freezing but it was still cold. Yet, staring out the window kept me in a zone.

"Here's your drink." I took the red wine and sipped on it thinking about Meek. It's been a few weeks and I missed him like crazy. Not to mention, all the times I've pleasured myself with thoughts of him.

"Your appetizers miss." A guy placed them on the table. I pushed the mushrooms to the side until they cooled off. The last time, I burned my tongue really bad and felt the effects for a few days. I picked a nacho up and bit down. The sauce dripped down my face and I felt someone wiping it off.

"Meek." He smiled as he stared down at me.

"How did you know I was here?"

"I own this and everyone knows who you are. Why you think they sat you here?"

"Because you aren't here."

"Nah. They know what time it is. Can I sit?" I pointed to the other seat. Instead of sitting across, he sat directly next to me.

"I miss you ma." He turned my face to his and placed the most tender kiss on my lips. I put the wine down, sat on his lap and rested my head on his shoulder.

"I missed you so much. Meek, you don't have to love me and I'm not settling but I don't want to be without you."

"You've never been without me. I'm around, just not in your presence. I know everything you're doing." I stared at him. Why is he watching a woman he isn't with?

"Can we at least be friends? I miss talking to you and the way you call me corny."

"We could never be friends." I rose off his lap and sat in my own chair. He scooted the chair closer and took my hand in his.

"We can't be friends because I'm in love with you too. Therefore: calling one another friends isn't a good.-" I jumped on his lap again and slid his hands in my pants.

"Oh you're gonna play with my dick in front of all these people?" I turned and the place was pretty crowded.

"As long as yours is the only one I'm playing with, who cares?" His hands gripped my ass while he grinded my hips in circles on his hard dick.

"I want you so bad Meek." I sucked on his bottom lip.

"Let's go." He lifted me up, adjusted himself and told the people to wrap my food up and we'd return shortly. Well it's not exactly how he said it. His version was more of, *wrap my girl shit up and it better be done by the time I get back.*

"You are so mean."

"I'm not mean but I do need the staff to be on their feet at all times."

"If you say so. Where are we going?" He removed my shoes and had me walk on the cold sand.

"Let me show you something real quick." We stepped under the boardwalk and there was no one around. He unbuttoned his jeans, slid them and his boxers down, pulled my pants down, turned me around and pushed himself inside.

"I missed this tight, gushy pussy. Mmph."

"And I miss this big dick tearing my insides up." I held onto the boards holding the pier up and started throwing it back for him. He placed his hand around my throat and made me extremely nervous. I had to remember he likes it rough and would never intentionally hurt me.

"I love the shit outta you C." With his hand remaining around my neck, he pulled me close and tongue kissed me.

Even with my body twisted and the cold weather, nothing could bring me off this cloud he had me on

"I love you too baby. Awww shoot." I allowed my body to succumb over and over to him and once he did the same, we put our clothes on and sat there. His arms were around my waist and his chin on the top of my head.

"I wasn't sure it was lust or love which is why I didn't tell you at the time."

"It's ok Meek."

"No it's not because you left upset and I didn't even check on you and I apologize for it." I tilted my head to look at him and he pecked my lips.

"You are amazing, weird and sexy."

"I am." I had to play a little coy.

"Yup. I love how genuine and loyal you are to everyone around."

"Yea well, I wish my sister was the same." He turned my body around.

"Shak told me what happened and Teri foul as hell for it. I get she wanted to help her friend out but it shouldn't have been done at your expense. Everyone knows you two don't get along so I'm not sure why she didn't think of that."

"Am I being a baby about it? Should I be ok with it since it's her floor and I gave her free range?"

"Would you be ok with me cheating on you?" I gasped because the thought made me nauseated.

"Exactly! You learned a lot from your ex and one of the things is, you're not gonna allow anyone to walk over you again. If she's mad then tell her to buy a different building and hire whoever she wants." He held my face in his hands.

"C'Yani don't let anyone; including me make you feel bad about the choices you make. You have the right to be comfortable anywhere you go without worrying about how its gonna make the next person feel."

"I miss us talking." He smiled and hugged me tighter.

"That pussy too sore for more making up?"

"It is but I'm willing to feel the mixture of pain and pleasure again if it's coming from you."

"Good. I have a room at the Ocean Place Hilton. It's under both of our names. Go take a shower, get comfortable and I'll be there to handle that."

"Why were you staying in a room?"

"Actually, today I was coming to see and take you there. It just so happens my staff called and told me you were here."

"Really?"

"Yes really. I missed the fucked outta you C'Yani Bailey." I cheesed extremely hard. I had no idea he missed me, as much as I missed him.

"Wait! Why aren't you coming with me?"

"My pops is calling me back to back which he never does. Let me check on him and I'll be right there."

"Be careful." He carried me up the sand and walked me to the car.

"I'll see you soon." We kissed again and I pulled off. I couldn't wait until I'm lying in his arms again. You never miss a good thing until it's gone. I pushed him away but I'm glad he returned that's for sure.

****

274

"Hi my name is C'Yani Bailey and I need the key to my room." I asked the person at the front desk.

"You didn't get one when you checked in?"

"My man checked in and left the key for me."

"Oh ok. I don't mean any harm. I'm just asking because most people give the other person staying the key." The woman stared at me.

"It's fine." I wasn't giving her too much information because its none of her business and why is she asking me anyway. Who cares?

"Do you need me to show you ID?"

"No ma'am. If a person tells you their name and a key is here for them we usually give it with no questions asked."

"That doesn't seem safe." She chuckled a little.

"This hotel is very expensive and we don't get people here who aren't supposed to be. Therefore, the need to ask is unnecessary."

"Ok. I guess."

"Here is your key and per the notes on this account, your man did something very special for you."

"He did. Oh my God. I'm so excited. See, we broke up and just got back together. I planned on doing something nice for him but he beat me to it. I'm so sorry. I don't mean to bother you with my mess." I blurted out forgetting I just told myself not to tell her my business. I took the key and smiled.

"Honey if your man can get you this excited, then make sure you give him something special too." She smiled and pointed to the elevators.

I stepped on with excitement. I wanted to know what he did? Would I like it? How did he get it done so fast? It's all a mystery and I couldn't wait to slide the key in the door. Once I did, my eyes grew wide. There were bags from Gucci, Prada, Giuseppe, Louboutin and others.

I shop in these stores here and there but never had this much stuff at one time. I looked in a few and there were shoes, purses, clothes and I noticed a card on the bed.

"To the woman who opened my eyes to a whole other world. You are truly special and I don't ever plan on letting you go. I love your bougie, non-fighting but can fuck me good

ass. This is just the beginning C'Yani and I can't wait to spoil you even more.

I put the card down and started crying. All these years wasted on Ty and God finally placed a good man in front of me. Crazy, hood and aggressive but good to me.

I stood and went in the bathroom to find rose petals at the bottom. When I turned the water on they began to float. There was soft music playing and a tv in the wall where the tub was. Oh yes, this is an expensive hotel.

After my bath, I threw on a hotel robe and laid on the bed. The news was on and I dosed off, only to wake up to a presence next to me.

"Meek!"

"Nope." I couldn't tell the voice and jumped up.

"Who are you and…" I stopped after noticing something on the other side of the room. It was another person. Is this part of the surprise Meek had for me? When I saw the bat, my eyes grew wide and all I kept praying was for Meek to make it here in time to save me.

"I'm pulling up now." I told my grandfather on the

phone. He asked if I heard from my father because he was

supposed to stop by and its not like him to do a no show.

I was shocked because he had been calling my phone

back to back and it's not like him. Unfortunately, I was making

love to my woman under the boardwalk so I couldn't answer. I

told him I was here and would have my father call.

I stepped out my truck with a smile on my face thinking

about C'Yani. I was happy to be in her presence and becoming

a couple again. I know it sounds corny but she had a way of

making me do corny things with her. She's the calm to any

storm I endure.

"What up?" I walked in and instantly became pissed

seeing Kim sitting at the table. She had a grin on her face,

which means the bitch is up to no good. The real question is,

why is she here?

"Tha fuck you doing here?" She came to me and ran

her hand up and down my chest. I grabbed her wrist and bent

them back.

279

"Bitch, don't play with me. Why you here and where's my pops?"

"He's outta commission right now." I dropped her hands and started searching the house for him.

"Outta commission?" I was confused.

"Let me show you." I followed her upstairs and found my father lying in bed with handcuffs around his arms and legs. His eyes were closed and I could see him barely breathing. He was covered but you could tell he may have been naked.

"Now we're gonna be together." She's still delusional as fuck.

"Pops, you ok?" I ran to him but her words stopped me.

"You see that bitch you fell for is cheating on you." She opened a phone and I heard someone moaning.

"Your bitch ain't thinking about you." She turned the phone and there was C'Yani in a video riding Ty. I'm assuming it's him because she ain't the type to sleep around.

"That shit could be old."

"I don't think so." I snatched the phone out her hands and I'll be damned. There sat the bags I brought her in front of the bed.

"And you left me for her." I was livid because not only did we just fuck, how the hell she fucking another nigga in the hotel room I rented? I couldn't wait to get my hands on her. I wasn't gonna let Kim know how bad it hurt to see that shit and changed the subject.

"Why the fuck you got my pops handcuffed?" I looked around for the keys.

"I wanted to see if he could fuck me as good as you." I snapped my neck to look at her.

"What the fuck you say?" I tried to remove the handcuffs but she had the keys jiggling in her hand.

"You heard me."

"Hold the fuck up! You fucked my pops?" She had a smile on her face like it was cute.

"He definitely has a big dick and made me cum a few times but his touch isn't like yours." I took my gun out and shot the bedpost to let his arms down.

"Pops you ok?" I smacked his face a few times to wake up. His eyes opened and he had a sad look.

"You have to kill her." He managed to get out and she heard him.

"That's why you're in the position you're in. Do you know your father called me crazy while I was riding him? Oh but he wasted no time cumming inside me. Meek you and I are gonna be pregnant because I'm ovulating and..." I turned and took a shot. I only got her in the arm and went to shoot again but my father called me.

"I need an ambulance." I had no idea what he was talking about because he looked fine. It wasn't until I moved the covers and he had what appeared to be stab wounds all over his body.

"SHIT!!!!" I call 911 quick and found some towels to keep the blood from pouring out. The comforter was so dark, I never noticed the blood.

"Hang on pops. They're coming." As bad as I wanted to get that bitch I couldn't because the 911 operator told me to apply pressure until the EMT's arrived.

"Meeeeeeekkkkkkkk. How can you shoot me? What if our baby got hurt?" I ignored her and pressed down as hard as I could to try my best at making sure he didn't die.

"Ahhhhh fuckkkkk!" I felt something sharp being impounded in my back.

"Bitch, are you fucking crazy?" I stood and used every bit of energy I had to strangle her. Whatever she left in my back, went in further as she kicked me in the nuts and pushed me against the wall, to get me off.

"Look what you made me do." I could hear the ambulance or some sirens in the distance.

"I'll be back to check on you baby. I need to get this bullet out my shoulder and check on our baby." She kissed my lips and shortly after my eyes closed. If I make it outta here alive, I'm gonna kill her and C'Yani.

To Be Continued…

Made in United States
Orlando, FL
12 October 2022